SOMETHING OF VALUE

Enrique Olmedo, lying naked, bloody and bound in his luxurious drawing-room at Westerton Old Hall, had forty-two knife wounds in his body and only the last was lethal. But who had tortured and killed him, and why? One person who might have known was Melissa Lloyd, ex-stripper and girlfriend of Mr Olmedo, but she had vanished. Mr Sanchez, cousin of the murdered man, thought the police were dragging their feet, so he called in the Peking Inquiry Agency and Sam Grant was put on the case . . .

Books by James Pattinson
in the Linford Mystery Library:

WILD JUSTICE
THE TELEPHONE MURDERS
AWAY WITH MURDER
THE ANTWERP APPOINTMENT
THE HONEYMOON CAPER
STEEL
THE DEADLY SHORE
THE MURMANSK ASSIGNMENT
FLIGHT TO THE SEA
DANGEROUS ENCHANTMENT
THE PETRONOV PLAN
THE SPOILERS
HOMECOMING
BAVARIAN SUNSET
STRIDE
FINAL RUN
DEAD OF WINTER
SPECIAL DELIVERY
BUSMAN'S HOLIDAY
THE SPAYDE CONSPIRACY

JAMES PATTINSON

SOMETHING OF VALUE

Complete and Unabridged

LINFORD
Leicester

First published in Great Britain in 1978 by
Robert Hale Limited
London

First Linford Edition
published 2003
by arrangement with
Robert Hale Limited
London

British Library CIP Data

Pattinson, James
Something of value.—Large print ed.—
Linford mystery library
1. Private investigators—Fiction
2. Detective and mystery stories
3. Large type books
I. Title
823.9′14 [F]

ISBN 1–8439–5064–2

Published by
F. A. Thorpe (Publishing)
Anstey, Leicestershire

Set by Words & Graphics Ltd.
Anstey, Leicestershire
Printed and bound in Great Britain by
T. J. International Ltd., Padstow, Cornwall

This book is printed on acid-free paper

1

Where it Happened

'That's the place you have to go to,' Mr Peking said. He pushed a slip of paper across the desk. 'Mr Sanchez will be expecting you at three o'clock this afternoon. That should give you ample time to get down there.' He sat back in his leather-upholstered chair and stroked his silky black beard with fat pink fingers, as though stroking a favourite cat.

Sam Grant picked up the paper and read the address written on it in Alexander Peking's own hand, which was surprisingly small and neat for a man as massively constructed as the head of the Peking Inquiry Agency undoubtedly was. Grant sometimes wondered just how much his boss weighed in the buff; which was a mental picture calculated to stop one in one's tracks in itself. Eighteen stone? Twenty perhaps? Maybe even more. He was certainly not the grey-hound type, or even the blood-hound for that matter. But there was no reason why he should be; he did none of the leg work; he left all that kind of thing to others while he sat in his comfortable chair in his comfortable office and pulled the strings. And that, from his point of view, was a very good arrangement indeed.

Grant read through the address twice: Old Hall, Westerton, Suffolk. There was an oddly familiar ring to it.

'That seems to strike a chord.'

'It should,' Peking said. 'It was in all the papers a few months ago. That's the place where Mr — or ought I to say Señor? — Enrique Olmedo got himself very thoroughly carved up.'

Grant remembered it then; it was the sort of crime that was bound to make the headlines. For a time. Until people got bored with it because nothing more seemed to be happening; no sensational arrests, no new and startling revelations, no developments of any kind. The police had apparently come to a dead end and the thing had gone cold. People had lost interest, forgotten about it; the general public had a very short memory.

Yet there had been a lot going for it at the outset; it had had all the right ingredients for a good story. The way Grant remembered it, Mr Olmedo, a wealthy South American businessman, had owned Westerton Old Hall for about a couple of years; he had modernised it, built a swimming-pool, and generally tarted the place up. Nobody in the village seemed to know a great deal about him, but they knew he came down to Westerton from time to time, never staying for very long, never taking any part in local affairs; a somewhat mysterious man with a mysterious background. But rich; oh, yes, undoubtedly rich. And perhaps with the tastes that a rich man could afford to indulge. There had been a lot of stories of Bacchanalian goings-on, of nude bathing in the pool, of midnight revelry; the stories had probably lost nothing in the telling, gathering considerable embellishment from vivid imaginations.

And then one morning Mr Olmedo had been found with his wrists and ankles tightly bound, stark naked on the carpet of his elegant drawing room, very bloody, very badly sliced up, very much alone, and with not a flicker of life left in him.

Grant remembered something else. 'There was a girl involved, wasn't there?'

Peking nodded. 'Name of Melissa Lloyd. Worked as a stripper before Olmedo took her under his wing. From all accounts he was really gone on her. Men of his age — fifty or so — are vulnerable that way.'

'Men of any age,' Grant said.

Mr Peking emitted a gusty sigh, admitting a regrettable but universal weakness. 'That is so.'

'Was he married?'

'Apparently not. May have had a wife back home where he came from. Who knows?'

'Miss Lloyd was supposed to have been with him the night he was killed, wasn't she?'

'Yes. But she vanished. The police haven't been able to trace her. They'd very much like to have a talk with that young lady.'

'I'll bet they would. She could probably help them quite a lot with their inquiries, as the saying goes. And how did we get involved?'

'Mr Sanchez rang up. He said he was looking for a good private investigator and this agency had been recommended.'

'Somebody must like us,' Grant said. 'Who is Mr Sanchez and what's he doing down at the Old Hall?'

'It appears that he is Mr Olmedo's heir and successor or executor or something. He's a cousin, so he said, and was in business with Olmedo.'

'What kind of business?'

'He didn't say.'

'Why does he want a private investigator?'

'He didn't say that either. Some people like to hold their cards very close to their chests. Maybe he thinks the police are dragging their feet and wants to get things moving. The case has been hanging fire rather a long time.'

'Solving murder mysteries isn't our business.'

'Anything is our business,' Mr Peking

said, 'if somebody is willing to pay for the service.'

'Except divorce.'

'One must draw the line somewhere,' Peking said.

Grant was not at all sure they ought not to draw the line at sniffing into murders as well, especially the particularly savage kind of murder that had caused Mr Enrique Olmedo to shuffle off this mortal coil at the ripe old age of fifty or thereabouts; but he decided not to say so. Peking would have thought he was being faint-hearted. And Peking could well have been right.

'So he gave no hint of what he might have had in mind?'

'None at all. He just said he wanted a first-class man.'

'So you immediately decided to send me.'

Peking lifted his heavy shoulders in a laboured shrug and allowed them to fall again to their natural position. 'You're the only one available; everyone else has a job in hand.'

Grant saw that he would get no

compliments from Peking. He had not expected any; compliments from that quarter were very few and far between; possibly because Peking thought that if he became at all lavish with praise an employee might get ideas above his station and even start asking for an increase in salary. When it came to forking out money Alexander Peking was about as eager as a man going to his own execution.

'Well,' Mr Peking said, 'that seems to be about all, unless you have any further questions.'

'Plenty of questions, but maybe I'd better keep them for Mr Sanchez.'

'It might be best.'

The telephone on Peking's left began to ring. He stretched out a hand and lifted the receiver. Grant decided it was time to leave.

* * *

He had lunch in Newmarket and then drove without haste to Bury St Edmunds. It was a pleasant June day, dry and sunny but not too hot for comfort, and the Cortina which he had recently acquired was a distinct improvement on the old Hillman which had seen far too many years of service and was long past its best. Peking had been complaining for some time that it was bad for the agency's image to have one of its investigators going round in a vehicle that was fit only for the scrap-heap. He had told Grant that he ought to get a newer car, and Grant had told him that he might consider doing that if Mr Peking could see his way to putting up some of the purchase price. It had taken Peking a long time and much heart-searching before he had been able to see his way, but finally his concern for the firm's image had won an exhausting battle with his parsimony and he had forked out.

Grant had taken the money without a qualm, since it was his opinion that the agency ought to supply a car anyway; but Peking had never seen things in that light; he felt that a man who used his own car would naturally be inclined to look after it more carefully. He told Grant not to tell any of the other members of the staff about the accommodation in the matter of the Cortina because it would only tend to make them dissatisfied, and he could not go round buying cars for all and sundry.

'By Jupiter, I'm not made of money, you know.'

Grant knew nothing of the kind, but he had been discreet about the Cortina deal. He appreciated the fact that he had received favoured treatment; which just proved how much Peking really thought of him.

About ten miles on the other side of Bury St Edmunds he turned left on to a minor road and was soon in what might have been termed the heart of rural England. It was not altogether unfamiliar, since he had been born and had spent the early years of his life in that part of the country. If things had worked out differently he might well have been a farmer rather than a private investigator, but there was not much point in thinking about that now.

Westerton was the kind of village that

made its appearance gradually — first an outlying farmhouse and some adjacent cottages, then a sinuous quarter of a mile of road, a few clumps of trees, a herd of Friesian cows grazing in a meadow, some more cottages, a church with a square tower and a graveyard full of headstones, ancient and modern, a cluster of old houses, an inn with a signboard on which was depicted a rather gloomy-looking white lion, a small shop, a garage with two petrol pumps, a duckpond with a lot of green weed growing on the surface, some newer houses with small front gardens fenced in by white-painted horizontal boards nailed to short posts, and then you were past the hub of the place; you could get through it in less than a minute if nothing got in the way. It took Grant more than a minute because he stopped to ask where the Old Hall was. The man who directed him was slightly deaf and he had to repeat the question twice before it got through. When it did a kind of gleam came into the man's eyes, which were a trifle rheumy with age, and he seemed to take more interest in his questioner.

'Ah, you'll be meaning where there was that there murder time back.'

'Yes,' Grant said. It was apparently still fresh in the minds of the locals; which was hardly surprising, since an event of that description was not likely to be forgotten in the space of a few months; it had certainly been gruesome enough to impress itself firmly on even the least retentive of memories.

The man licked his lips as though savouring anew some piquant taste. 'That were a rum ol' do, that were.' He gave a laugh, high-pitched and cackling. 'Ain't every day o' the week we get a murder down here like.'

Grant could believe that. A village the size of Westerton might easily wait another five hundred years before anything quite as exciting ever occurred again; always supposing it remained untouched by urban overspill and development, that certain death to all things pleasantly rural.

'You a policeman, then?' the man asked. He had a sprinkling of grey stubble on his chin and a thin neck like a plucked turkey's. 'Ain't had no policemen askin' questions for a tidy while now.'

'You still haven't,' Grant said. 'Just tell me how to get to the Old Hall.'

'Newspaper, then?' The rheumy eyes stared at him intently. 'One o' them there London newspapers. Givin' it another write-up, are you?'

'No. And I'm not a journalist. Look, do you mind directing me or should I ask someone else?'

'You can ask anybody you like,' the man said. 'They'll tell you the same. Take that next turning.' He pointed. 'Half a mile down the lane, I reckon. On the right. Got some big iron gates. Lawyer?'

'Wrong again,' Grant said. He set the car moving and left the man to his speculation. The first guess had been nearer the mark, but he saw no reason why he should reveal his business to anyone who happened to question him about it. Possibly there would be some discussion on the subject in the White Lion that evening, but it was of no consequence.

There was a row of beech trees on each side of the lane, their branches meeting overhead to form a leafy roof. Grant drove the Cortina at a modest speed and met no traffic. The gates were about ten feet high; they were set back from the road, hung on stone pillars which had lichen growing on them. They were standing open and he drove through without stopping. It was ten minutes to three.

There was a longish driveway skirted by grass and trees, and the house, when he came to it, was not quite as large as he had expected. It had probably been built a couple of centuries ago and had weathered nicely. There was a lot of creeper festooning the walls and the paint was in good condition. He parked his car on a square of gravel in front of some steps leading up to a stone porch and a heavy oak door, and he could see the swimming-pool about twenty yards from the house on the right. It seemed, he thought, to strike a false note with its brash modernity in that setting. There was no one using it, though the weather was just right for that kind of thing. He tried to imagine what it had been like in Olmedo's time: those parties, beautiful girls in bikinis, or no bikinis, laughter, gaiety, noise. It was silent now, silent and deserted; no more riotous parties, no more lovely girls. No more Olmedo.

He walked over to the pool and looked down into the water. Already there was evidence of neglect: some sediment on the bottom, a few twigs and leaves floating on the surface, a kind of green slime on the tiles round the edge. He crouched down and dipped a finger in the water; it was chilly in spite of the sunshine.

A man said: 'You are thinking of taking a swim, Mr Grant?'

Grant stood up and turned without haste. He was not startled; the man had made very little noise in his approach, but he had detected that faint sound and had been prepared. The man had come to a halt about five yards away; he was of rather less than average height, but fleshy, dark-haired, dark-skinned, with a small black moustache; in his middle forties,

Grant would have said, and somewhat out of condition; he was probably too indulgent with his appetites and took too little physical exercise.

'I am correct in supposing that you are Mr Grant?' His English was good, but it was easy to tell that it was not his mother tongue.

'Correct,' Grant said.

'It was a simple deduction of course. I have been expecting you. I am Guido Sanchez. But you, for your part, will have already deduced that.'

'It seemed probable.'

Sanchez extended his hand. It was soft, but the grasp was firmer than Grant would have imagined. Sanchez did not prolong the handshake; it was an act of politeness, nothing more; there was no warmth in it. There was no detectable warmth in his eyes either as he gazed into Grant's face; a shrewd assessment perhaps but nothing else. Grant was not looking for anything more than that; it was a business appointment and there was no reason why Mr Sanchez should take an instant liking to him, or even pretend to do so. Whether or not he was satisfied with what he saw in Grant's face, it was impossible to judge; his expression gave nothing away.

'Mr Peking assured me that you are a most competent investigator.'

'I do my best,' Grant said.

'That is not quite the same thing.'

'True. But it would hardly be worth while my telling you how good I am. I don't suppose you would consider that an entirely unbiased opinion.'

Sanchez smiled briefly. 'A practical demonstration would certainly be more convincing. But at least I can see for myself that you are satisfactory from the purely physical point of view.'

'I always hope that matters won't become too physical when I am working on a case,' Grant said.

'And in your experience has that hope always been fulfilled?'

Grant admitted that it had not.

'But you are still alive.'

'I've managed.'

'Yes.' Sanchez took another appraising look at him, then turned away. 'Let us go into the house. Come.'

Grant followed him. Guido Sanchez had a waddling kind of walk and slightly splayed feet. He was dressed in a suit of a quality Grant could never afford to buy; it was pale grey and looked really expensive; the tailor had used all his considerable skill to iron out the defects in Sanchez's figure, but no one could have been entirely successful in that respect; some blemishes simply could not be disguised.

They went in by the front door. There was a fairly spacious entrance hall with a wide staircase ascending from it. It was cool in there; Grant felt the chill immediately he stepped inside. He got the impression of an old house no longer lived in, no longer warmed by human occupation, human relationships.

'I will show you where it happened,' Sanchez said. He walked to a door on the right and pushed it open. 'This way, Mr Grant.'

It was a large room with a high ceiling and tall windows looking out to the front and the side. Grant could see his Cortina parked on the gravel and the trees beyond it. In the room were some richly upholstered chairs and a sofa, an antique china cabinet with some fine-looking pieces in it, and other expensive items of furniture. There was an Adam fireplace capable of holding half a hundredweight of coal at one filling, in front of it a high brass fender with brass tongs, shovel and poker, each three feet in length. The mantelpiece was of marble and there was a marble clock on it stopped at twenty-five minutes past seven. Which probably had no significance whatever.

'That is where he was found.' Sanchez pointed down at the carpet. His voice had hardened. 'My poor cousin Enrique. We were boys together in Lima; we grew up together. And this is where they found him.'

The carpet had been cleaned, but there would always be the mark on it where Olmedo had bled; there had been no need for Sanchez to point out the spot where the body had been found; Grant could have discovered it for himself.

'He was murdered,' Sanchez said.

'Brutally and foully murdered.' He stood facing Grant across the patch of carpet which still bore indelible evidence of the crime. 'And you, my friend, are going to find out who did it.'

2

The Key

'It's not really my line,' Grant said.

Sanchez looked at him in faint surprise. 'What isn't?'

'Murder.'

'But Mr Peking assured me that you had had considerable experience with murder cases.'

'Oh?' Grant said. He saw how it was: Peking had been selling him as some kind of all-purpose Sherlock Holmes. He might have expected as much; Peking would not hesitate to sell him as anything if there was money to be made out of the sale. He wondered just what kind of price Sanchez had been persuaded to pay for his services. A pretty steep one, no doubt; pretty damned steep.

'Are you saying this is not true?' Sanchez asked.

'No, I'm not saying that.'

'So?'

'So I still wouldn't call it my line.'

'Never mind what you would call it.' Mr Sanchez sounded a trifle impatient. 'Just tell me whether or not you are going to work for me. If not, it seems we have both been wasting our time and I must find someone else.'

Grant could imagine what Mr Peking's reaction to that would be. He would be displeased, very displeased indeed; and the effect of his displeasure might be to cause a great deal of friction all round. Grant decided that it might be best to avoid upsetting Mr Peking and to go along with Sanchez, at least for the present. Maybe if things became too sticky he could pull out later, though he was none too sure about that; once you got yourself involved in a case of this sort it was not always easy to become uninvolved. Still . . .

'It's a police job really,' he said. 'In this country the police like to handle their own murder inquiries. They don't take kindly to outsiders poking a finger in the pie.'

'Police!' Sanchez gave a snap of the fingers in contemptuous dismissal of the entire force. 'What have they done?' Have they found my cousin's murderer? Have they brought him to justice?'

Grant could hardly argue that they had. In the face of such complete failure on the part of Scotland Yard it would have been difficult to convince Sanchez that the British police were indeed a very efficient organisation. He wanted results, and the results had certainly not been forthcoming — yet.

'Perhaps if you were to give them a little more time — '

'Time! How much do they need? They have had time enough. Now I must take action myself. I have no more patience left, you understand?'

'I understand.'

'Good. I am pleased to hear it.' Sanchez became somewhat cooler. He invited Grant to sit in one of the armchairs and he himself sat in another. 'Now let us talk about this matter. You said, Mr Grant, that murder was not your line. May I ask what is?'

'Well, it varies. Almost anything, I suppose.' That was true. He had even done a stint as a bodyguard to a lady; but he hardly felt inclined to mention that; it was not really his line either, and it had ended up as a murder case anyway. 'The field is pretty wide.'

'Give me an example.'

Grant answered at random. 'I'm sometimes hired to find missing persons.'

'Ah!' Sanchez appeared interested. 'And you are good at that?'

'I've had some successes.'

'Then I think this case may not be so far out of your line after all. It is a missing person we have to find. That is the start. The rest stems from that.'

'You are talking about Miss Lloyd of course,' Grant said.

Sanchez nodded. 'Miss Lloyd is the key, don't you think? If we could only talk to her we might discover so much that we need to know.'

'You think she was here when Mr Olmedo was killed?'

'I am sure of it.'

'So it's a case of find the lady.'

'Undoubtedly it is.'

'That may not be too easy. The police have been trying and they haven't managed it.'

'So you must do a little better than the police. Do you think you can do that?'

'I can try.'

'Try hard, Mr Grant, try very very hard.'

'And if I find the lady, what then?'

'Then you let me know at once.'

'The police will want to know too.'

'The police can wait. It is not they who are employing you; I am. And I wish to have a little heart-to-heart talk with our Miss Lloyd.'

Grant had an uneasy feeling that Sanchez might be planning to take the law into his own hands; he might be soft physically but there was a certain hardness in his eyes which gave the lie to that outer softness; there could well be quite a lot of steel below the surface and it was certain that he meant to exact retribution for the death of his cousin. Perhaps only a very personal vengeance would satisfy him; perhaps he believed in the biblical eye for an eye and saw himself as the avenger of blood. Grant was none too happy with the prospect of getting mixed up in anything of that kind, but perhaps it would never come to it anyway; no point in jumping fences before you came to them. The girl had yet to be found.

'I believe your cousin's body was discovered by a woman who worked here,' he said.

'Mrs Jenner. She is still looking after the house. Eventually I shall sell it, but for the present — until this business has been satisfactorily cleared up — I shall keep possession. I feel the answer could still be here, within these walls.'

Grant doubted that but did not say so. He said: 'I should like to have a word with Mrs Jenner.'

'Of course,' Sanchez said.

'Alone.'

'Alone?'

'She may talk more freely if there is no third person present.'

Sanchez shrugged. 'If you think so.'

* * *

Grant talked to Mrs Jenner in the kitchen over a cup of tea. She was a middle-aged, homely person with a solid, capable look about her, and she answered his questions frankly and freely. It appeared that Olmedo had employed her more or less in the capacity of housekeeper, but she had never slept in the house.

'Jenner — my husband, that is — he wouldn't have liked it, you see. Stands to reason, don't it?'

'Didn't you have any help? It's a large house.'

'There was a girl chance times. And Mr Olmedo wasn't down here only now and then. He had his other place up in London, see.'

'But I understand he had parties, guests staying here — '

'Oh, yes, there was that. Young ladies mostly; very flighty. A few men. Had high old times, they did.'

'Didn't that make rather a lot of work for you?'

Mrs Jenner shook her head. She had fair hair, rather fluffy, beginning to lose its colour in places, pale blue eyes and an ample chin. 'Lor' bless you, no. He got extra help for the occasion.'

'From the village?'

'No. They come down with him from London. Foreigners.' Mrs Jenner's lips pursed up after she had spoken the word, as though it had left a nasty taste in the mouth. Apparently it was all very well for the master to be foreign, but servants were a different matter. 'I didn't have much to do with 'em. Used to leave 'em to it.'

'But there were no guests or servants here the night Mr Olmedo was killed?'

'No. Except Miss Lloyd, and you couldn't hardly call her a guest, could you?'

'No?'

'Well, I mean to say, they was that close. Proper sweet on her, he was; you could see that. Never seemed to bother much with parties after he took up with her. Seemed like he'd lost interest in other women.'

'What would you say her attitude to him was?'

'Oh, she liked him. Well, he was a

likeable man, even if he wasn't English. I wouldn't say she was in love with him, not the way he was with her; but that's understandable, them being so different in age and all. Still, I'd say she liked him well enough.'

'So you don't think she killed him?'

'Her!' Mrs Jenner looked amazed and even shocked at the suggestion. 'Whatever gave you that idea? Lor' bless you, she wouldn't never have done that to him. Why should she?'

'Why do you think she ran away?'

'Frightened,' Mrs Jenner asserted with conviction. 'Frightened, poor little soul.'

'She's still not been found. Do you think she's still frightened? After all this time.'

'Why not? Maybe she saw the murderer and maybe he saw her. So maybe she's afraid he'll kill her to keep her from telling on him if she don't keep hidden away.'

'Why didn't he kill her at the time, then?'

'Well, I don't know. Maybe she was too quick getting away and he couldn't catch her.'

'Did she leave her things here?'

'No. She took everything.'

'That doesn't look as if she was running from the murderer. Not if she had time to pack her bags and take them away with her.'

'Well, like I told you, I don't know.' Mrs Jenner sounded faintly irritated. 'I'm not a detective. You work it out for yourself.'

Grant sipped his tea and complimented Mrs Jenner on the excellence of the brew in an effort to mollify her. She accepted the olive branch and offered a plate of biscuits. Grant took a custard cream, a favourite of his, and munched it with enjoyment. The kitchen had been modernised; it gleamed with stainless steel and chromium plate. A refrigerator hummed gently as though crooning to itself and an electric cooker waited in silence for further duty.

'What was she like?' Grant asked.

'Miss Lloyd? Oh, a sweet little thing. Pretty as a picture. Good figure, too; but of course she would have, seeing what she'd been doing for a living. Not that I hold that against her. Everybody's got to manage as best they can, and if that's what you've got, why not make the most of it?'

'You liked her, then?'

'There wasn't nothing to dislike about her. She didn't put on airs and was as friendly as you could wish. Used to come in here and have a chat with me when she'd got nothing better to do, same as what you're doing now.'

'Did she tell you anything about herself?'

'A bit. Told me as how she hadn't got no relations; not as she knew about, that is. Been brought up by Dr Barnardo's, seems like.'

'She wouldn't have any family to go to, then?'

'Oh, no.' Mrs Jenner gave Grant a calculating look, not altogether trusting. 'You're going to try to find her, I suppose?'

'She ought to be found — for her own sake. To clear things up. She can't stay in hiding for the rest of her life.'

'Will she be in trouble? With the police, I mean.'

'I don't see why she should. If she's done nothing wrong.'

'Like what?' Again there was a certain stiffening in Mrs Jenner's attitude. It was obvious to Grant that she was all on Melissa Lloyd's side.

'Like being mixed up in what happened to Mr Olmedo, for instance.'

'You can put that idea out of your head,' Mrs Jenner said. 'That's like I told you — she wouldn't hurt nobody, least of all him. I mean to say, where would be the sense in it? He'd have done anything for her; she only had to ask. He even give her a car.'

'A car?'

'One of them little sports models, it was. Red.'

'How do you know he gave it to her?'

'Because she told me. Didn't make no secret of it. She was pleased with it. Like a toy to her, it was.'

'You haven't any idea where she might have gone?'

'No. I told the police. They wanted to know. I told them I couldn't help them at all, not in that way. As far as I know, she might have gone anywhere. And good luck to her, I say.'

Grant drank some more tea. He saw that he was not going to get much out of Mrs Jenner. If she did know anything that might have helped in the search for Miss Lloyd she was evidently not going to divulge it. But he was inclined to believe that she was telling the truth; it was more than possible that she had no more of a clue to where the girl had gone than anyone else.

'I believe it was you who found the body, wasn't it?'

'Yes.' Mrs Jenner's mouth closed up tightly again. It was probably not a pleasant recollection.

'What time would that be?'

'About half-past eight in the morning.'

'That would be the time you came to work, I suppose.'

'Then you'd suppose wrong. I started about eight.'

'And yet you didn't find the body until half-past! How was that?'

'I was busy in here. I keep a key to the back door and I let myself in that way.

First thing I do is get things going back here afore I trouble about the other part of the house.'

'It didn't surprise you not to hear anyone moving about?'

Mrs Jenner gave a laugh, though she looked and sounded unamused. 'Why should it? They never got up afore ten; sometimes later.'

'I see. So it was half an hour before you went to the drawing room?'

'About that. I couldn't swear to the exact minute.'

'Of course not. And that was when you found Mr Olmedo?'

'Yes. The door was standing open and I just looked in. I didn't see him at first because the curtains was drawn and there was that big old sofa in the way; but I could see something had been going on all right. There was things knocked over and that, like there'd been a fight or something. I thought, there'll be some clearing up to do in here, and then I went into the room and pulled back the curtains to let the light in, and when I turned I see poor Mr Olmedo and the blood and all.' Mrs Jenner shuddered histrionically. 'Horrible, it was. I felt sick.'

'I can imagine,' Grant said. 'It must have been a great shock to you.'

'Give me a rum old turn, I can tell you. Like I says to Jenner, I wouldn't want to start every day of the week with that sort of thing. Between me and you and the table here, Mr Grant, I wouldn't be surprised if that's took ten years off my life; not a bit surprised, I wouldn't.'

'Let's hope it's not quite as bad as that, Mrs Jenner.'

'You may hope,' Mrs Jenner said darkly; but it was apparent that she herself had written off those ten years and saw no likelihood whatever of winning them back from a malignant fate. 'You may well hope.'

'And what did you do then?' Grant asked.

'Well, I could see as how there wasn't nothing I could do for him, so I went and looked for Miss Lloyd. I called, but there was no answer. The house was in a state, I can tell you, like somebody had been hunting for something, pulling out drawers, opening cupboards, throwing things on the floor, making a high old mess.'

'Hadn't they been in the kitchen as well?'

'Well, yes, but I didn't give it much thought. You see, Miss Lloyd would sometimes do a meal in the evening and she wasn't the tidiest of persons in that respect. So I just thought she'd made a bit more clutter than usual. Anyway, I went upstairs and into the bedroom where they used to sleep, and it was the same there; bedclothes all anyhow, wardrobes standing open, but no Miss Lloyd. And then I see her stuff had all gone, everything, and I knew it was no use looking for her no more. Still, it was a relief in a way; I'd been afraid I might find her like him, if you see what I mean.'

'I see what you mean.' It must indeed have been a relief to Mrs Jenner. Two bodies in one morning would have been rather too much of a bad thing. 'So then, I take it, you called the police?'

'Yes. I didn't touch nothing. Well, you're not supposed to, are you? I just used the telephone and then come back here to the kitchen and made myself a good strong cup of tea. I needed it.'

'I expect you did.'

It seemed to be about all. Mrs Jenner had told all she knew and it amounted to very little. If she had been present at the time when the crime had been committed she might have had a great deal more to tell, but she had been half a mile away; everything had happened long before her arrival on the scene.

Grant stood up. 'Thank you, Mrs Jenner. You've been very helpful. And thank you for the tea.'

He found Sanchez still in the drawing-room, standing with his hands in his pockets and staring moodily out of one of the windows.

'This is a dreary place,' he said. 'I can't think why Enrique bought the house.'

'From what I've heard, it seems he made it cheerful enough when he came down here.'

Sanchez frowned. Perhaps he disapproved of that kind of thing. 'Did you get what you wanted?'

‘I got as much as I expected,’ Grant said.

‘But no lead to where the girl may have gone?’

‘No. I’ll have to work that out the hard way.’

‘Don’t take too long about it.’ Sanchez walked over to a side-table and picked up a photograph frame lying face downward. ‘This may help.’

Grant took the frame and looked at the photograph. it was signed across the bottom right-hand corner: ‘With all my love, Melissa.’

‘So this is Miss Lloyd?’

‘Yes.’

Grant was rather surprised that the police had not taken the photograph; but perhaps they had plenty of others and did not need it. It was just the head and shoulders, semi-profile, a dark-haired girl, smiling. He could see why Olmedo had been attracted.

‘You may as well keep it,’ Sanchez said.

Grant unfastened the back of the frame, took out the print and slipped it into his pocket.

'I'll be on my way, then.'

Sanchez walked with him to the car. 'And remember,' he said. 'I talk to the girl before the police get their hands on her.'

'You want me to bring her back here?'

'I shall not be staying down here.' He handed Grant a card. 'That is my London address and telephone number. You had better get in touch with me immediately you find her.'

'If I find her.'

'I am relying on you, Mr Grant. Please do not fail me.' He sounded very earnest.

'Okay, I'll let you know as soon as anything turns up.'

'We'll work something out from there. Perhaps you'll bring her to me — if she's willing. Or perhaps I'll come to you.'

'As you wish, Mr Sanchez,' Grant said.

He started the Cortina and left Sanchez standing on the gravel. He wondered why the man should be so insistent on talking to Miss Lloyd himself. Was it because he no longer trusted anyone else to get the truth from her? The truth that might lead to his cousin's murderer. Or was there some other reason? He tried to think of another reason and nothing came up; so maybe it was after all simply a burning desire for vengeance. Again he felt a shade uneasy at the prospect, but again dismissed the uneasiness with the argument that it was no concern of his what Sanchez did or did not do. First things first, and there could be no doubt what the first thing was: it was find the lady.

And that perhaps was more easily said than done.

3

Lay Off It

It was too late to report to the office when Grant got back to London, so he went straight home to the flat. He found Susan Sims there; which was not altogether a surprise, since she was living with him again.

'Hello, Tham darling,' she said. 'Did you have a good day?'

Without waiting for him to tell her whether he had had a good day or a perfectly lousy one, she flung her arms round his neck and kissed him with considerable enthusiasm and every sign of thoroughly enjoying the exercise. Grant enjoyed it too, because Miss Sims was not the kind of person who made kissing a penance. Not for him, anyway. Far from it.

When she had disengaged herself from the embrace he looked at her and thought, as he had thought many times before, that she was very nice to come home to. She was a darling and maybe some day he would succeed in persuading her to marry him. He had not managed it yet, but he would work at it and perhaps eventually she would agree to sink her principles and really do it.

Not that he had anything to complain about as things were at present, except that every now and then she would come to the conclusion that some of the gilt had worn off their relationship, and she would pack her bags and take off for fresh woods and pastures new, or whatever the equivalent was in her vocabulary. He had no idea where she went and he never asked. She had a family of some kind up in Nottingham, but she was not on the best of terms with them and he was pretty sure she never went there. And, anyway, she always came back after a time. At least, she always had so far, and he hoped she always would, because the place was never the same without her; it was cold and empty and about as cheerful as a morgue. She might be as crazy as a coot, she might be years younger than he was, she might speak with that ridiculous lisp, but somehow he had never got tired of her; for him the gilt never wore off. He needed her around, that was the fact of the matter, and when she was not there he missed her like hell. So maybe he was really in love with her. And maybe there was no maybe about it. No, sir.

'I love you, Tham,' she said. 'Do you know that, you big brute?'

'Are you sure, sweetheart?'

'Of courthe I am, thilly. Goodneth me, I've known you long enough to be thure, haven't I?'

'That's true. But you've cleared out a few times and left me comfortless.'

'Now,' she said, pouting a little, 'you aren't going to throw that in my teeth, are you?'

'I wouldn't throw anything in your teeth,' Grant said. 'They're a lovely set of snappers and grinders and I wouldn't want to damage them. Why do you love me?'

She pondered the question, frowning slightly like a child trying to work out a sum. Then: 'I don't know, Tham. You're not terribly handthome, tho it can't be that.' She put her head on one side, giving him a careful inspection. 'Of courthe, you're very well made. I mean, you haven't got any flab, have you? No thoft tum to carry around and wobble like a jelly. Thtill, a girl wouldn't fall in love with a man jutht becauthe he didn't have a jelly belly. Maybe we have a union of the mind.'

Grant laughed. 'Maybe we have.'

'Not,' she added, 'that we don't have a union of the body too. That'th very important, ithn't it? The phythical mutht be allied to the thpiritual to produthe a perfect and thatithfying harmony of the thoul.'

'Good God!' Grant said. 'What have you been reading?'

'Nothing. I heard it on the radio.'

'You shouldn't believe everything those disc jockeys tell you. They get their material out of Christmas crackers. Is there anything to eat? I'm starving.'

She was not a bad cook in a slapdash sort of way, and she had a meal dished up in practically no time at all. She shared it with him, eating about one mouthful to his four.

'You didn't tell me what you've been doing today,' she said. 'Anything thrilling?'

'Nothing thrilling. Just a trip down into Suffolk.'

'Thuffolk! Whatever for?'

'To see a man.'

'What did the man want?'

'He wants me to find a rather elusive young lady.' Grant took the photograph from his pocket and laid it on the table. 'That lady.'

She looked at the photograph, and she had the frown going again. 'I don't know that I want you to find her, Tham.'

'Why on earth not?'

'She'th too pretty.'

'What's that got to do with it? It's just a job.'

'It'th never jutht a job when you go looking for pretty women. You get emotionally involved.'

There was a grain of truth in that, Grant thought; and maybe even more than a grain. But he did not say so.

'What do you want me to do? Refuse the job? It's my living, you know.'

'Why don't you make a living thome other way?'

'Like what, for instance?'

'Oh, I don't know. There mutht be plenty of other thingth you could do.'

'Possibly.'

'Tho why not give it a try?'

'Maybe I'll do that one of these days.'

'But not now?'

'Not now.'

She looked again at the photograph and read the inscription. 'Who ith Melitha?'

'She's a Miss Lloyd and she used to be a stripper.'

She frowned again. It had perhaps been a mistake to tell her that. It was bad enough hunting for a lady; hunting for a stripper, or even an ex-stripper, was worse. 'Who wath the love for?'

'A man named Olmedo who is now dead. He was murdered.'

'Murdered!' Her eyes opened wide and he could see that she was more disturbed by this revelation than she had been even by the idea of his tracking down a stripper. She got up and came round to his side of the table and looped an arm round his neck. 'I don't like it, Tham. Why do you have to get micthed up in murder?'

'I told you — it's a job.'

'You could get yourthelf killed.'

'Nobody's going to kill me. Why should they?'

'You've nearly been killed before.'

'And I'm still alive and kicking. I'll be all right, don't worry. Nobody's going to bother about me.'

'How can you be tho thure? Thomebody killed the man, didn't they?'

'That was different. Anyway, I'm not hunting for the murderer; I'm hunting for Miss Lloyd.'

'Why?'

'Because I'm being paid to.'

'Who'th paying?'

'A man named Sanchez. He wants to talk to her.'

She unwound her arm from his neck and went back to her chair. But she still looked worried. 'I don't like it, Tham. I have a prethentiment.'

'Now,' he said, 'let's not have any of your presentiments. It's just imagination, you know. Nothing's going to happen to me, nothing at all.'

The assurance failed to cheer her; she continued to be depressed. After a while he began to feel a bit depressed himself. He even wondered whether there might not be something in that presentiment of hers, and he thought there just might at that. It was turning out to be a pretty miserable sort of evening, one way and another.

* * *

In the morning he called in at the office in Blunt Street to give Mr Peking a progress report. Not that there had been any progress to speak of.

He had left Susan Sims no more happy about the assignment than she had been the night before. She had had the cards out, and the cards had been unpropitious — so she said. He was not sure whether she really believed in all that junk, but she pretended to, and she made it an extra argument in trying to persuade him to abandon the search for Miss Lloyd.

'It'll only turn out badly.'

He thought that was quite possible, but not because the cards said so.

Mr Peking wanted to know what kind of man Mr Sanchez was. Grant provided a brief description.

'He's a Peruvian. He and Olmedo were brought up in Lima. He seems very much put out by his cousin's murder and annoyed with our splendid British police for not having laid their hands on the murderer. He said he wanted me to find out who did it.'

'Ah!' Mr Peking said; and waited.

'I told him it wasn't my line of country.'

Mr Peking frowned. 'I don't think you should have said that.'

'It was the truth.'

'Perhaps. But there was no need to make a parade of it.'

'I didn't make a parade of it. I just told him. Anyway, we came to a compromise. I'm to find the girl and he's going to take it from there.'

Mr Peking looked relieved. He had obviously feared that a client might be slipping off the hook and was glad to find that it was not so. 'What exactly do you think he meant by taking it from there?'

'I had the impression that he hopes to get a lead from Miss Lloyd to whoever killed his cousin.'

'And then?'

'Then I rather think he intends to skip the formalities of a trial. I could be wrong, of course, but from the way he talked it certainly pointed in that direction.'

Mr Peking looked faintly worried. 'I hope he won't do anything as foolish as that. He could find himself going to gaol.'

'Maybe he thinks he could get away with it.'

'They all think that.'

'And a lot of them are right.'

Mr Peking gave a sigh. 'Unfortunately, that is so. But it's a risk, a very grave risk. If Mr Sanchez is thinking along those lines you had better make sure you're not involved.'

'I have no intention of being involved. I

haven't the same personal motives as our client has.'

'It would be so bad for the reputation of the agency.'

'I was thinking more of my own welfare.'

'Well, naturally,' Mr Peking conceded, though with some apparent reluctance, 'you have to take that into account. Nevertheless, I trust, as a loyal employee, you will always remember that your prime duty is to do nothing which might bring the Peking Inquiry Agency into disrepute.'

'Like getting myself jugged for complicity in a murder, for example?'

'Especially that.'

'I'll bear it in mind. I certainly wouldn't want to tarnish the image now that I've got a new car.'

Mr Peking seemed uncertain whether or not to regard this as taking the mickey, but Grant maintained a guileless expression and he decided to let it pass.

He said. 'Would you consider Mr Sanchez to be a trustworthy man?'

Grant gave the question some thought

before making a reply. Then: 'Apart from his obsession with vengeance, yes, I'd say he was. Certainly I've no reason to suppose otherwise.'

'Well,' Peking said, 'we got his cheque in the post this morning, so at least we won't be out of pocket if he runs off or does anything else foolish. That's always supposing the cheque doesn't bounce.'

'I don't think it'll bounce. And I don't think he'll run off.'

'No, it's hardly likely. Still, it's always as well to have some money in hand. It promotes confidence.'

Grant wondered just how large a cheque Sanchez had sent in the interests of promoting confidence, but he did not ask. There was never much point in asking questions you knew would not be answered.

* * *

Detective Sergeant Edgar Walden drank some of the beer which Grant had paid for, set the mug down and wiped his mouth with the back of his hand.

'So you're working for Mr Sanchez,' he said. 'Why?'

'Because he's paying.'

'That isn't what I meant. I meant why pull in the Peking circus?'

It occurred to Grant that Mr Peking would not have been altogether pleased if he had heard his organisation referred to as a circus by Detective Sergeant Walden, who was a rugged sort of character with a lot of police service under his belt and the jaundiced view of life that habitual dealing with criminals tended to produce. But he did not say so to Walden because he knew that he would only have got a derisive laugh for his pains.

'Mr Sanchez seems to think that the police have not been making enough progress. He thinks it's time somebody came up with some answers to the question of who killed his cousin, Mr Olmedo.'

'And he thinks that one ex-copper like you can do what we, with all the vast resources at our disposal, haven't managed to do?' Walden was sneering a little; maybe rather more than a little. 'He must be weak in the head.'

'He didn't strike me that way.'

'No? Well, I'll tell you this, Sam, you won't make yourself very popular with Kerrison if you go poking your nose into his case.'

'I'll try not to tread on Detective Superintendent Kerrison's toes,' Grant said. 'Actually, all I'm trying to do is locate Miss Lloyd.'

'Why?'

'Mr Sanchez would like to have a talk with her.'

'He's not the only one. Do you think we haven't been looking for her?'

'I'm sure you have. But you haven't found her, have you? I don't see what harm there can be in my having a go.'

Walden grunted. He took another swig of beer and gazed round the bar, turning his jaundiced eye on one person after another, as though seeing in each a prospective candidate for the handcuffs and the statutory warning. He had never been a close friend of Grant's; a one-time colleague in the early days of their careers, but that was all; not exactly buddies.

'What do you want to know?' he asked.

'What you know,' Grant said.

'You've got a bloody nerve, mate.'

'Well, can you tell me something about Miss Lloyd? Where did she work?'

'Stripping, you mean? The last place was the Deuce of Diamonds in Levy Street. You can try there, but it'll be a waste of time.'

'I've got to start somewhere.'

'That was where Olmedo picked her up. I don't expect she took much persuading to give up a glittering career and go away with him. Money's a strong argument.'

'How did he make his money?'

'He was in the import-export line. Seems your Mr Sanchez managed the South American end of it. When Olmedo handed in his chips Sanchez came over to this country to take charge of things.'

'So he wasn't here when it happened?'

'No. He'd been over recently, but he'd gone back.'

'Import and export could cover a wide field of activity.'

'It probably did — and does — but

that's not our pigeon.'

'Unless it has a bearing on the murder.'

'You'd better leave it to us to figure that one out,' Walden said. 'You concentrate on the lady.'

'Why do you think she beat it?'

'I don't have an opinion on that,' Walden said.

Grant did not believe him.

'I suppose she could have gone away with the killer — willingly or otherwise.'

Walden shook his head. 'No.'

'How do you know?'

'She took her own car. A red MGB two-seater. Present from Olmedo, so I heard.'

Grant decided not to tell Walden he had heard the same thing. 'That should have been easy to pick up.'

'It wasn't. She had several hours start and she must have gone to earth before the alarm was put out. She could have travelled a long way in that time in a car as nippy as that one.'

'And you've got no idea where she might be holed up?'

'If we knew the answer to that, do you

think there'd be any job for you?'

'I suppose not. How about motive for the killing? Any lead on that?'

'Work it out for yourself. Olmedo had been stripped naked and there were forty-two knife wounds on his body, very widely distributed, hardly any part that hadn't had some attention from the blade.'

'Somebody went berserk?'

'I wouldn't say so.'

'Oh?'

'All the wounds except one were very carefully inflicted. They would have caused a great deal of pain but not death.'

'I see,' Grant said. 'What you're telling me is that it was a case of torture.'

'That's what it looked like.'

'To make him talk?'

'It's the usual reason.'

'So why kill him?'

'Maybe he did talk, and after that he was no more use so he was silenced — for good.'

'Was anything taken from the house?'

'We can't be sure about that. The housekeeper didn't think anything had gone, though there were obvious signs of a hurried search. But she might not know all there was in the place. Those characters were not after the usual kind of loot — pictures, silver, that junk; they had something else in mind, something Olmedo had got hidden away.'

'They? So you think there was more than one?'

'Well, what do you think, mate? Olmedo was hardly likely to sit nice and still while one man carved patterns on his flesh.'

'But I understood his wrists and ankles had been tied.'

'That's so. But it's pretty difficult for one man to tie up another man against his will unless he gives him a tap on the head first. There was no evidence that Olmedo had been tapped on the head.'

'Okay, so we've got more than one assailant. Maybe they just wanted to kill Olmedo. A vendetta.'

'So why go to the trouble of tying him up? Why do the fancy knife work?'

'Sadism. Punishment. Revenge for something he did back home in Peru.'

'What you're suggesting is we should be looking for some fellow countrymen of his?'

'It seems a possibility.'

'We thought of it. We already have followed that line and it didn't get us anywhere. Look, Sam, you know what murder cases are like. There's the easy ones that practically solve themselves — the local boys manage them without ever calling us in; then there's the difficult ones you have to grind away at till you finally come up with the answer; and last of all there are the real bastards that you never are going to work out. This could be one of them; it has plenty going for the killers — an isolated house in the heart of the country, probably not a soul awake anywhere around, nobody to hear Olmedo yelling out when they put the knife in — '

'Except Miss Lloyd.'

Walden nodded. 'Except Miss Lloyd — who we can't find.'

'Fingerprints?'

'Those boys were professionals. They probably wore gloves.'

'That would make tying knots difficult.'

'They could have taken them off for that. Anyway, there weren't any dabs, apart from the housekeeper's and Olmedo's and the girl's.'

'How did you identify Miss Lloyd's?'

'Deduction and elimination.'

'You hadn't got them on file?'

'No; she's never been in trouble.'

'She could be in trouble now.'

'So could you,' Walden said. 'My advice to you is, lay off it. Those jokers who operated on Olmedo are the wrong sort of people to tangle with; they play rough. If you get too near them — and I'm not saying I think you ever will, mind — but if you do they might give you a bit of their unwelcome attention. You don't want to get carved up, do you?'

'Not particularly.'

'So take my advice, mate, lay off it.'

Grant smiled wryly. 'To be perfectly frank with you, Ed, I'd be glad to, but I have to earn my bread and cheese.'

'Bread and cheese is no use to a dead man,' Walden said.

4

One More Thing

It was a mean little room with linoleum on the floor and some flaking brown paint on the walls. There was scarcely any furniture apart from an upright piano, two or three folding chairs and a card-table. There was a woman sitting at the piano, middle-aged, sharp-featured, bored. A dark, greasy-haired man in a striped shirt and pale blue trousers was sitting on one of the chairs, a chewed-down cigar stuck in the left-hand corner of his mouth.

'Mr Cowan?' Grant said, trying to make himself heard above the sound of the piano without actually interrupting what was going on.

The man shot him a sidelong glance, quickly appraising. 'That's me. Wotcher want?'

'A word.'

'Word! What word? Carncher see I'm busy?' He had a heavy, pockmarked face, moist lips and a croaking voice. The cigar waggled in his mouth but stayed there.

'I think perhaps you can help me.'

'Help you! So I'm a charitable institution? No, not that way, Shirley, for crying out loud. Like I told you, like I told you.'

The last remark was addressed to a blonde girl who was going through a strip routine to the accompaniment of the piano. She was doing it without any visible evidence of enthusiasm, and she was even smoking a cigarette at the same time. Grant wondered whether the cigarette was part of the act; it could have been a new gimmick.

'I'm not looking for a hand-out,' he said. 'Just some information. About a girl named Melissa Lloyd.'

Cowan's head swivelled again. 'Are you a copper?'

'No. My name's Grant. I'm carrying out some inquiries for a client.'

'A private eye. Look, I already had the fuzz on my back, must be months ago. I told them all I know, and that wasn't a lot.'

'I believe she worked here at one time.'

'Melissa? Sure, she worked here for a while. Before she shacked up with that rich dago what got hisself knocked off. But I don't know nothing about her private life. I don't trouble myself about where the girls come from, what they do with their spare time, where they go. You think I don't have troubles enough without that? I told the fuzz, I don't know nothing.'

'I'm just trying to find her,' Grant said. 'I'd be glad of a lead, anything — '

'I told you — '

The blonde girl was taking off her left stocking, balancing on her right leg, cigarette smoke getting into her eyes. She began to cough and lost her balance. Cowan jumped up from his chair and made a rush at her.

'No, no, no! Stop it! Stop right there! So I gotta show you. So I gotta teach you every damn thing. Play us that bit again, Gertie.' He pushed the girl aside.

The woman at the piano went back and

started playing it over again. Cowan, with surprising agility for a man who had so obviously allowed himself to run to seed, went through the motions of the stocking routine. It was a grotesque mime; it was also very funny. Grant laughed.

The blonde girl said: 'Maybe you should do it on the stage, Mr Cowan. You'd be a wow.'

Cowan stopped what he was doing and glared at her. 'You're so damned smart.' The sharp-faced woman was still hammering away at the piano keys as though she had a grudge against them, and he had to raise his voice almost to a shout. 'Knock it off, Gertie, carncher!'

The music stopped abruptly. Gertie gave a toss of the head and sat with her hands in her lap, waiting resentfully for further orders. The blonde girl was still smoking the cigarette; she was standing with one elbow resting on the top of the piano, wearing a bra and a pair of skimpy briefs and one stocking. She was well built, but in a few more years, Grant thought, she could be running to fat unless she watched the calories like a miser. But maybe by then she would have found somebody like Enrique Olmedo to take her under his wing and make further work unnecessary. Or maybe she would be doing one-night stands at stag parties and rugby club dinners, and hating it.

'Okay, Cowan said, 'let's pack it in for now. We'll work something out. You better get dressed, Shirley.'

The blonde girl gave a shrug, gathered up the articles of clothing she had shed and went out through a doorway at the back of the room. The sharp-faced woman closed the piano lid with a bang and followed her out.

'It's a dog's life,' Cowan said.

Grant wondered what kind of a dog led that kind of life. 'You could try something else.'

'I could starve, too.' Cowan took the cigar out of his mouth, looked at the soggy end with an expression of disgust, seemed in half a mind to throw it away, but finally put it back where it had come from. 'So what's all this about Melissa Lloyd?'

'I just want to find her, that's all.'

'Okay, you find her. And when you do, tell her from me there's a job waiting for her back here. I'm not saying she was anything classy, but compared to that one — ' Cowan gave a jerk of the thumb in the direction of the doorway through which the blonde girl had departed and made an expressive grimace. From which Grant gathered that he was not feeling altogether pleased with Shirley just at that moment.

'I'll tell her that,' Grant said. 'If I find her. But she seems to have vanished.'

'Maybe somebody killed her like they killed that Olmedo. Dumped the body in a pit.'

'I hope not. A dead body would be no use to me.'

'Nor me neither,' Cowan said. 'Though, come to think of it, some of the bodies I get around here might almost as well be dead. So the coppers haven't found her?'

'No.'

'You think you can do better than them?'

'I'm trying.'

'Well, I'd help you if I could, but it's

like I said, I don't know a thing about her background. For my money she was just a doll that took her clothes off.'

'No ideas?'

'Nothing.'

'Well, thanks for giving me some of your time anyway. I won't keep you any longer,' Grant said. He turned and walked to the door.

Cowan wished him luck. 'And if you do find her, remember what I said. Now that rich dago is dead she could be in need of a job.'

'I'll remember,' Grant said.

He was about fifty yards away from the Deuce of Diamonds when the blonde girl caught up with him. It was outside a Greek restaurant and he was glad to see that she was more respectably clad than when he had last seen her; even in the streets of Soho a bra, a pair of almost non-existent briefs and one stocking might have attracted some attention as the complete walking-out gear for some-one like her.

She had been running and her breathing was slightly more rapid than normal. 'Don't be in such a hurry,' she said. 'I could maybe help you.'

Grant stopped. 'In what way?'

'You're looking for Melissa, right?'

'Right.'

'I used to work with her.'

'At the Deuce of Diamonds?'

'No; it was before she went there. Look, why don't you buy me a cup of coffee? We could talk about it.'

Grant looked at his watch; it was coming up to one o'clock. 'Why don't I buy you lunch?'

'If you like,' she said.

They chose the Greek restaurant because it was there. The blonde girl had a healthy appetite and Grant wondered whether he ought to warn her about what the calories might do to her in a few years' time if she went on shovelling it in regardless. But it was none of his business, and maybe she was just giving herself a treat because she liked Greek cooking and it was free.

'I'm Shirley Waters,' she told him. 'I didn't catch your name.'

'Sam Grant.'

'You're a genuine private eye?'

'I'm an inquiry agent.'

'Okay, call it what you like. Why do you want to find Melissa?'

'That's what I'm being paid to do.'

'Who by?'

'Does it matter?'

'Well, what I mean in this. Is she going to be in trouble if you find her?'

'I see no reason why she should be. In fact it would probably be best for her if she was found by somebody like me. There could be other people looking for her who might be a lot more dangerous; people who ought to be behind bars.'

'This is all mixed up with that murder, isn't it?'

'Yes.'

She chewed a piece of mutton — or it might have been goat; by the time meat got to the table it was not always easy to tell. She gave him a long hard stare. Then finally she said: 'Okay, Sam, I think you're honest. You look honest anyway, so I'll take the risk.'

'You do know something that would help?'

'It may and it may not. As I said, I used to work with Melissa a while back. It was in a crummy little joint called the Peel of Belles.' She spelt it out so that Grant could get the play on words. 'Can you beat that? Some guys must sit up nights working these things out.'

'Poetical,' Grant said. 'You were friendly with her?'

'You could say that, I suppose. She was a nice kid. There aren't many in this business I'd give the time of day to, but she was different from most. She'd had some rough patches, too. When she was thirteen some man persuaded her to run off with him. He was forty and a real bastard; he used to lock her in his caravan which he kept hidden away in some wood. The things he made her do — a kid of thirteen. They ought to hang men like that. In the end she managed to break out and get away. But they never found the man; he beat it.'

'She never knew her parents?'

'Never. I'll bet they were right bastards too. When she was seventeen she came up to London to try her luck. Well, don't we all? At eighteen she was living with this photographer who worked for one of the soft porn magazines. She modelled a bit for him, but it didn't last. He was a pig.'

'Did you tell all this to the police?' Grant asked.

'I haven't talked to the police. How did you get the idea I had?'

'They went to the Deuce of Diamonds. They questioned Mr Cowan.'

'That was before I worked there. Anyway, I wouldn't tell anything to those pigs. They never did anything for me except bad things.'

'You've had trouble with them?'

'They've pushed me around a few times.'

Grant did not ask why the police had thought it necessary to push Miss Waters around. It was not her story he wanted. He said: 'This is all very interesting, but I don't see that it's going to help me find Miss Lloyd.'

'I'm coming to that. Don't rush me. You're trying to figure out where she could have gone into hiding after she lit out from that house where she was living with Olmedo. Right?'

'It seems to be the most likely approach.'

'Well, I don't know; it's just a thought, but she could have gone to this commune, couldn't she?'

'Which commune?'

'It's some place she was at for about a year before she threw it up and came back to the city glitter. She had friends there and I think she had a hankering to go back some day; to the simple country life and all that jazz, which I don't mind telling you would drive me up the wall.'

'Why didn't she go?'

'Well, there was a lot pulling the other way, wasn't there? She wasn't one to despise money. Maybe in a way she was a sort of split personality, if you see what I mean.'

'You think it was because of the money she went to live with Olmedo?'

'I don't know; I never met him. Maybe she was fond of him even if he was a lot older than her. It wouldn't have been like that swine that picked her up when she was only thirteen; he was a pervert.'

'So you believe she may have gone back to the commune?'

'I don't know. But she never talked about any other friends, not that I recall.'

'She needn't necessarily have gone to friends.'

'No, but it's possible, isn't it? Have you got anything better to go on?'

Grant admitted that he had not. 'Where is this commune? Did she tell you?'

'She told me, but I've forgotten.'

'That's a lot of help.'

Shirley Waters looked faintly aggrieved. 'You can't expect me to keep things like that in my head for ever. You'll have to nose around.'

'It's going to be a tall order hunting round all the communes in the country.'

'Oh, you don't need to do that. It's somewhere in East Anglia.'

'You're sure of that?'

'Pretty sure.'

It narrowed the field. It also made the thing more probable. An East Anglian commune would be within easier distance of Westerton Old Hall than one in another part of the country. In the MGB she could have reached it in an hour or two, maybe less. And what better place to go to for sanctuary? The kind of people who lived there might not even read the papers or listen to the radio; they might never have heard of the Olmedo killing. And even if she told them about it they might not go to the police; they had a different set of values from the ordinary citizen. She had been one of them and maybe they had their own loyalties. It might not come to anything but it was certainly worth following up; especially since it was the only lead he had.

'Is it any help?' Miss Waters asked.

'It could be, Yes, I think it could well be. I'm very much obliged to you.'

She had finished eating and was looking at him thoughtfully. 'Do you ever have any spare time, Sam?'

'Now and then.'

'Maybe you and me could have a little fun together sometime. What do you say, Sam?'

'Maybe,' Grant said; and he was thinking that Miss Sims would not have been at all happy if she could have heard the way this conversation was going. Shirley Waters represented just about everything that Miss Sims would least have wished him to come into contact with: she was blonde, attractive, voluptuous and almost certainly amoral. For the sake of Miss Sims's peace of mind he decided it might be best not to mention the fact that he had another stripper on his books, so to speak.

The girl seemed a trifle dissatisfied with his answer. 'Only maybe?'

'The fact is,' Grant said, 'I look like being rather fully occupied for a time.'

'And after that?'

'I'll be in touch.'

'Don't call us; we'll call you,' she said, with more than a hint of sarcasm. 'Okay, it was a nice lunch.'

* * *

Grant put in an appearance at the agency later in the afternoon. The two girls in the outer office seemed busy, but none of the other Peking agents was there, so no doubt they were all out earning their salaries with one kind of inquiry or another.

Lois stopped tapping her typewriter and glanced up at him. 'Easy day, Sam?'

'So so.'

She patted her hair coquettishly. 'Are you taking me out to dinner?'

'Not tonight, my lovely. I have other duties to perform.'

'I bet.'

'He's got a date,' Vickie said.

'He's always got a date. It's the glamour that attracts them like wasps to a jam pot.'

'What glamour?' Grant asked.

'The dirty raincoat, the felt hat with the turned-down brim and the cigarette attached to the lower lip.'

'I've had my raincoat cleaned, I never wear a hat and I don't smoke.'

'So it must be the personality.'

'Or his handsome face,' Vickie said, and laughed.

They both laughed, so it must have been a joke.

'You should be careful,' Grant said. 'You could do yourselves an injury. Is His Lordship engaged?'

'There's nobody with him, if that's what you mean,' Vickie said. 'He's probably filing his nails.'

'He's a real old file,' Lois said.

They both laughed again; it seemed to be national laughter week. Grant left them to it.

Peking was not filing his nails, or anything else. In fact he was doing absolutely nothing when Grant walked in; he seemed to be meditating. But he soon came out of his meditation and brought his mind down to more mundane levels.

'Well?'

'I think I have a lead,' Grant said. 'It may not come to anything but it's worth a try.'

'Tell me.'

Grant told him. Peking gave it a run round his brain and decided that it certainly was worth a try. Seeing that it was all they had.

'I thought I'd go down there tomorrow

and ferret around. Not much point in starting today.'

Peking agreed. 'The young lady appears to have had a somewhat chequered career, one way and another. If you do find her you'll need to handle the matter with some delicacy. I suppose you understand that?'

'I'll be as delicate as I can,' Grant said.

'There's the question of the police, too. We don't want to do anything that might upset them.'

'We certainly do not.'

Mr Peking gave a faint sigh. 'On the other hand, we have to consider the interests of our client. We have a duty to respect Mr Sanchez's wishes.'

Grant knew what Peking really meant, though he would never have put it in so many words. He meant that as long as Sanchez was coughing up the hard cash they ought to do everything they could to keep him happy, without actually coming into collision with people like Detective Superintendent Kerrison and Detective Sergeant Walden. Which might entail the performance of a rather difficult balancing act by Sam Grant.

Still, it had not yet come to that, and maybe it never would. It all depended on whether or not he succeeded in finding Melissa Lloyd.

* * *

Susan Sims walked into the bedroom and stood with hands on hips, looking at him.

'What do you think you're doing, Tham?'

He had a holdall open on the bed and a clean shirt in his hand. 'I'm packing a few things.'

'You're going away?'

'I've got to go down to the country tomorrow. I may be gone a few days.'

'Looking for that thtripper?'

'She's not a stripper. Not any more.'

'Oneth a thtripper, alwayth a thtripper; that'th what I thay.' Miss Sims sounded very dogmatic on the subject.

'Well, you can keep on saying it, but I'll still have to go.'

'Why don't you take me with you?'

'I don't think that would be at all wise.'
'Why not?'
'You'd be a distraction.'
'You mean I'd be in the way. Ith that it?'
'I do have work to do.'
'Chathing a thtripper. Ith that what you call work?'
'I'm not chasing a stripper.'
'Then what are you doing?'
'Pursuing an inquiry.'
Miss Sims gave a derisive snort, which was rather unladylike but probably expressed her feelings more effectively than any words.
'You wouldn't enjoy it anyway,' Grant said.
'How do you know I wouldn't?'
'You'd miss the bright lights, the gaiety of the big city life.'
'What gaiety?' she said, her mouth going down at the corners.
He saw that it was going to be difficult to persuade her that she was likely to have a more delirious time of it if she stayed behind at the flat than she would if she accompanied him on his safari into the

wilds of Eastern England, so he gave up trying.

'We could thleep out under the wide and thtarry thky,' she said, with a dash of the poetical which he had never suspected she had in her.

For himself he had no intention of sleeping out under the wide and starry sky. It would probably be damned cold and might well rain. 'I gave up all that sort of thing when I left the Boy Scouts, so why don't you stop arguing?'

She sulked a little. 'Well, if you won't take me with you, you needn't ecthpect to find me waiting for you when you come back.'

He wondered whether she really meant it, and it made him a shade uneasy, because she might just be due for one of her walk-outs. So maybe he ought to take her with him after all. But he thought it over and came to the conclusion that it was simply not on.

'Now, Susie, darling,' he said, 'you don't mean that.' And he tried to kiss her, but she pushed him away.

'Don't Thuthie darling me, you meathly

thtripper-chather,' she said. 'And you'll thee if I mean it; you'll thee.'

Grant sighed. It was going to be just one more thing to worry about. As if there were not enough items in that line already.

5

Away From It All

She argued about it for half the night, so what with one thing and another he had a rather poor ration of sleep and set off in the morning feeling somewhat below his sparkling best.

They had breakfast together, but she kept warning him that it would probably be the last meal they would ever share and he had better make the most of it. And he was still wondering whether she was really serious, and very much afraid she might be, with the result that he got very little enjoyment out of mopping up the fried sausage and egg, or even the toast and marmalade. Which was a pity, bearing in mind the price of such commodities these days.

'Where will you go if you leave me?' he asked.

'I'll find thomewhere. Don't let that bother you.'

'You'll have to work for a living.'

'Do you think it ithn't work looking after a thlob like you?' she demanded.

He had never regarded it in quite that light. 'I thought you loved doing things for me.'

'Huh!' she said.

'I don't want you to go.'

'Why don't you treat me with thome conthideration, then?'

'I thought I did treat you with consideration.'

'You're a male chauvinitht pig.'

'Oh, God!' he said. 'Don't tell me you've gone all Women's Lib.'

'It'th about time I did,' she said darkly.

But she was very loving when he said goodbye and she kissed him quite passionately. The trouble was, he could not be sure whether it meant she had decided not to leave him after all or whether it was by way of being a last fond farewell.

'See you soon,' he said.

'Huh!' she said. 'You'll be lucky.'

Which was pretty enigmatic, he thought, and not exactly reassuring.

* * *

There appeared to be more communes in East Anglia than he had expected; they seemed to be growing in popularity as more and more citizens got fed up with the rat race and decided to go back to the simple life. There were urban communes and rural communes, but he thought he might as well skip the urban kind, since Miss Waters had said that the one where Melissa Lloyd had spent a year was in the country.

He made inquiries at local welfare offices, which were listed in the telephone directory, and was provided with addresses. The welfare people seemed to know quite a lot about communes, because apparently the drop-outs from the rat race never forgot their rights under the social security regulations and were pretty adept when it came to filling in forms and claiming any benefits that might be going. Or at least some of them were. In fact some appeared to have made such a close study of the subject that they never missed a trick; which was where they differed from the vast number of old-age pensioners and widows and deserted mothers, who missed a lot of tricks and went without what they might have had because they didn't know what they were entitled to, or how to fill in the necessary forms, or were simply too proud to ask for what was theirs by right. The commune dwellers thought that sort of pride was just a lot of hogwash. And maybe they were right at that.

Grant decided to limit his search for a start to the counties of Suffolk and Norfolk. By the end of the day he had covered a lot of ground and had learnt far more about communes and the type of people they attracted than he had known before; but he had picked up no scent of Melissa Lloyd. He was not far from Westerton, and he thought of calling in at the Old Hall and telling Sanchez how things were going, but he decided not to. There was, after all, very little to tell, and it was seldom a good idea to give the client an account of the way inquiries were being carried out: that could lead to nothing but argument and interference. Results were really all that counted, and the means by which they were obtained was best kept under the hat; the mystique of the business was something that counted for a lot in the eyes of the customer, even if it might in fact amount to no more than trudging round and asking questions. So, all things considered, best to give Sanchez a miss this time round. Besides, he might no longer be at the Old Hall; he had talked of returning to London.

Instead of going to Westerton, therefore, Grant headed for Bury St Edmunds and checked in at an hotel. It was not late, but he felt thoroughly fagged out and rather depressed in spirit too. Yet he had not really expected anything better to come of his efforts; the lead was slender and might well result in no trace whatever of Miss Lloyd being discovered. He had known that from the start and had accepted it. So why the depression? Well, maybe it was not the job that was causing it but the thought of Susan Sims packing her bags and shaking the dust of the flat from the soles of her dear little feet; the possibility that when he returned he would find the place deserted and cheerless. He thought about it while eating a solitary meal, and the result of this thinking was that after he had eaten he used the hotel telephone to put a call through to the flat. He hung on for quite a while, listening to the ringing tone and giving Miss Sims time to get out of the bath if she happened to be in it, but finally he had to come to the conclusion that she simply was not there.

He put the telephone back on the hook and went to the bar and ordered a beer and sat drinking it slowly. A lot of people seemed to be having a whale of a time, talking in loud voices and laughing and slapping one another on the back. He watched them with a jaundiced eye and brooded on that unanswered telephone in the flat in London. It proved nothing, of course: she might just have gone out for the evening; why the devil shouldn't she? He could hardly expect her to sit alone in the flat waiting for him to ring; it was not the kind of thing he did as a rule anyway. So why this time? And why let it bother him that the call should go unanswered? But it did bother him, and he rang again later. Again there was no answer. He went to bed having made no contact with her and he was convinced that she had walked out on him again.

He gave it another try after breakfast the next morning, and it was still the same ringing tone which he was beginning to hate. He let it go on for what seemed a hell of a time, because she might be asleep and he knew she could be hard to wake; but it was no use; he gave it up and went to the desk to pay his bill.

'Did you get through with your call?' the receptionist asked. She was a nice friendly girl with a nice friendly smile.

'I got through,' Grant said, 'but nobody answered.'

'Oh, what a pity. Later perhaps.'

'Yes, later.'

Perhaps.

* * *

It was still fairly early in the day when he put his bag in the boot of the Cortina and made a fresh start on the search for Melissa Lloyd. He decided to stick to that and forget about what Susan Sims might or might not be doing; he was not being paid to worry about Miss Sims.

It was getting on for noon when he drove the Cortina down a rutted, grass-grown lane between rampant thorn hedges interwoven with brambles and fringed with clumps of stinging-nettles and cow-parsley. He had crossed over into Norfolk earlier in the morning and was now well off the beaten track, if by the beaten track one meant roads classified as 'A' or 'B'. This was truly rural, the kind of countryside in which you might expect to stumble on a commune, far from the contaminating influence of the affluent society with its supermarkets and bingo halls and flyovers and central heating and double glazing, electric lawn-mowers and washing-up machines. This was where things were still primitive and nature started on the doorstep.

The house was built of clay lump, which was a local material that had gone out of use and had given way to mass-produced and characterless brick. The clay lump had a facing of plaster, except in places where it had fallen away to leave the clay exposed like raw flesh under the skin. If nothing were done about repairing the damage rain and frost would cause the clay to crumble and eventually the entire house might come tumbling down. There was a pantiled roof, the steepness of which indicated that it might once have been thatched, and there were dormer windows like elevated dog-kennels and a lean-to at one end which seemed to be buttressing the wall and preventing it from falling out. The paint on the woodwork was old and flaking, and the whole structure looked dilapidated and tired of it all.

There were some outbuildings, too — an old tarred barn with a switchback ridge, stables, pigsties, poultry sheds — and they all had the same look of dilapidation and neglect. There was a pond with some ducks swimming on it, and about a dozen children of various ages and both sexes were playing in the mud and sunshine, stark naked and not giving a damn about anything. There were three goats tethered to stakes and munching some coarse-looking grass, and they were not giving a damn either.

Grant brought the car to a halt and got out. He strolled over to the pond, and the kids paused in what they were doing and looked at him with some curiosity. They had a lot of mud on them and he reflected that there were undoubted advantages in letting kids run naked: skin was an easily washable material.

'What are you doing?' he asked.

A black-haired boy of about five answered. 'Fishing.'

He had a stick with some string for a line and a bent pin for a hook. The fishing looked to be sheer make-believe; it was not the kind of pond that was likely to have any fish in it anyway. The other kids seemed merely to have been digging in the mud and paddling.

'Caught anything?' Grant asked.

'Not yet,' the boy said, as though he

still had hopes. 'Who are you?'

'I'm Sam Grant. Is anyone at home?'

'We're at home,' the boy said.

'I mean is anybody in the house?'

'Yes.'

'I'll take you,' one of the girls said. She might have been about six. She reached out and took hold of his hand, transferring some of the mud. 'Come on.'

Grant allowed her to conduct him to the house. There was a door in the lean-to which was standing open, and with the small naked girl tugging at his hand he stepped into what appeared to be a kitchen. It was quite large and there was plenty of room in it for a plain deal table and some wooden chairs, a sink with a pump and a draining-board, and a Calor gas cooker. There were also two women.

'Excuse me for walking in like this,' Grant said, 'but I had a rather urgent invitation.' He glanced down at the small girl who was still clinging to his hand.

'Don't apologise,' one of the women said. 'People do just walk in. It's that sort of place, you know. No ceremony.'

‘My name is Grant.’

‘Sam,’ the small girl added.

‘All right, Sarah,’ the woman said. ‘Run along, darling. I’m sure Mr Grant can manage now.’

The child released his hand and sped away, leaving muddy footprints on the brick floor and more mud on his fingers.

‘I’m Moira,’ the woman said. ‘We don’t bother much with surnames.’ She was dressed in a long black skirt and a patterned blouse, nothing on her feet. She had chestnut hair, a bit tangled, as though she could hardly be bothered to comb it, and silver-rimmed glasses. She was quite young and might not have been at all bad-looking if she had taken a little trouble with her appearance. ‘If you’d like to wash your hands — ’ She went to the sink and pumped some water into a bowl.

There was a cake of yellow soap in an enamel dish. Grant washed his hands and dried them on a roller towel. The second woman had said nothing; she had long blonde hair and was wearing dark sun-glasses with large frames.

‘This is Joy,’ Moira said, introducing her.

Grant nodded. The woman looked at him but said nothing. She was dressed in denim slacks and a blue cotton shirt. The shirt was tight enough to reveal the outline of her breasts and he could tell that she was wearing no bra and had no need of one. She was standing on the other side of the table and there was a mixing-bowl in front of her. Her hands had flour on them and some of the flour had got on to her shirt and slacks; she was not using an apron. He wondered why some people wore sun-glasses even indoors; but it was all a matter of taste.

‘Are you selling something, Mr Grant?’ Moira asked.

‘No,’ Grant said.

‘I thought you might be a salesman. We get them occasionally, but it’s usually a wasted journey. We’re not big buyers; we manage without a lot of the things that most people look upon as necessities.’

‘I imagine so. You don’t happen to take in guests, I suppose?’

‘You’re not telling me you’re looking

for accommodation?'

'Would you be able to put me up if I said I was?'

She gave a laugh. 'What do you think? There are twenty of us, including the children. It's a big house but there isn't unlimited room.'

'So you never have guests?'

Her voice seemed to harden slightly. She looked at him with growing suspicion. 'What do you want? What are you asking?'

The blonde woman, the one named Joy, said nothing; but her hands had stopped moving; they were resting in the mixing-bowl, in the flour.

'I am asking whether you have a guest at the present time,' Grant said.

Moira gazed at him in silence for a few seconds; then said: 'How would that concern you?'

'I am looking for someone. A girl. That is, a young woman.'

'Why?'

'I think I might be able to help her.'

'Help her? In what way?'

'She's running away from something.

She can't go on running for ever. And there's no need. I want to tell her that. There really is no need.'

'What are you?'

'I'm a private investigator.'

'You're being paid to find this woman?'

'Yes.'

'Then it's not for her sake?'

'Not entirely. But she'll come to no harm. It'll be for her own good.'

'That's what you say, but she might not think so — whoever she is.'

'Her name is Melissa Lloyd,' Grant said.

Moira shook her head. 'There's no one here of that name. There are no guests; only the members of the commune.'

'I don't see any others.'

'They are out — working.'

'Oh, I see.'

'We do work, you know. We're not just idle layabouts.'

'I didn't say you were.'

'But you might have thought so. I think you had better go now.'

'So you can't help me?'

'To find a woman named Melissa

Lloyd? No. I'm sorry. You'll have to look somewhere else.'

'Yes,' Grant said, 'I suppose I shall.' He moved towards the door, then turned. 'You haven't seen a red MGB sports car around by any chance?'

She shook her head again. 'There are no cars here.'

'You have no transport?'

'We use a horse and cart. We like the old ways best.'

'We may all have to go back to them when the oil runs out.'

'It can't be too soon,' the woman said.

Grant thought she might well have a point there. He looked at the one with the blonde hair. She still had not moved, had not uttered a word.

'Goodbye, Joy.'

She turned her head towards him but still said nothing. He could not see her eyes because of the dark glasses. Perhaps living in the commune, away from contact with the madding crowd, she had become shy of strangers. He would have liked to see her without the glasses; she would have looked very lovely, he thought.

The children were still playing by the pond when he stepped out of the house. He strolled over and asked the boy who was fishing whether he had caught anything yet.

'No,' the boy said.

'What kind of fish do you usually catch?'

'Sharks, mostly,' the boy said.

Grant nodded. 'It looks a likely place for sharks.'

He walked back to the Cortina and got in. From the car he could see the stables. One of them had the door secured with a chain and padlock. He would not have expected that; in that kind of community locks and keys ought to have been discarded along with the other trappings of the bourgeois style of life. Here no one would steal anything; it was all common property. Or was it?

He started the engine, turned the car and drove away down the narrow lane, thinking.

⋆ ⋆ ⋆

Later in the day he put through another call to the flat from a telephone kiosk in a small village. Again he hung on for a long time, hoping; but there was no answer; no one picked up the receiver in the flat in London and said: 'Hullo, Tham darling; I'm glad you rang. I thtill love you.' There was only that damned ringing tone which could be the saddest sound in life when it just went on and on. He gave up waiting for her to get out of the bath or come out of the bedroom or wherever else she might be, and he knew that he had to accept the fact that she had gone; it would just be kidding himself to suppose otherwise. It had happened before and each time he had had to accept it; but each time he was a little bit older and he had to ask himself, was this the time she went for good and never came back? And he could not be sure of the answer; he simply could not be sure.

When he came out of the kiosk he was feeling depressed and he had an impulse to give up the search for Miss Lloyd and go back to London. That way he would certainly find out whether Susan Sims had really gone. But what good would it do? He could imagine how pleased Mr Peking would be to hear that he had allowed private matters to stand in the way of duty. Not that he cared two pins whether Peking was pleased or not, except that Peking represented the pay-cheque and he was not exactly keen on looking for another job.

So, all things considered, best not to go back to London. Best to get on with what he was being paid to do and try to forget about Miss Sims.

6

Someone to Lean On

He had booked no hotel room for the night; he was not expecting to have much time for bed, not if things went according to plan. He had snatched a few hours of sleep in the car, parked in the shade of some trees in a quiet corner where no one came to disturb his peace or ask him what he thought he was doing. In the evening he drove into Diss and had a meal and killed time as best he could until he was ready to go.

At eleven o'clock he was driving out of the town and by midnight he was again in the vicinity of the commune where he had spoken with the woman named Moira and had thought about the blonde woman in the dark glasses and the flour on her hands. He parked the Cortina in a gateway, took a torch from the glove compartment and walked the last two hundred yards or so down the narrow lane which led to the clay-lump house.

There was no light showing anywhere, but the moon was up and he had no difficulty in finding his way. He had seen no sign of any dogs on his earlier visit and he hoped there were none, because dogs could be the devil when you wanted to do a little quiet snooping; even if they didn't come at you and take a bite out of the fleshy part of your leg they were likely to set up an unholy din and waken everyone to the fact that there was an intruder around.

But he came to the pond and no dog had let out a howl or a whimper, and there was not even a quack from the ducks, so he supposed they were all safely shut up for the night. He walked over to the stables and he could hear a horse moving around in one of them; and then he was at the door with the padlock on it. He shone the torch on the padlock for a moment and it looked a simple type, not a Yale or anything as fiendish as that; so he put the torch away and took a piece of bent wire out of his pocket and got to work. After he had been at it for about five minutes without any tangible result he came to the conclusion that lock-picking was not his forte; so he let the padlock drop and the chain rattled and a dog began to bark.

So they had one after all. He almost decided to give up then and call it a day — or more accurately a night — but the dog appeared to be shut up and he was reluctant to go away without having accomplished anything, even if what he was doing did have a distinct flavour of illegality about it. The horse, as if taking its cue from the dog, was getting a bit more restive and was giving a nervous little whinny now and then, besides moving around in its stall and stamping on the floor to show it knew that something was going on.

Grant looked at the chain and he could see that it was looped through a big staple in the door and another in the jamb. It was the normal kind of stable door, made in two halves, with the upper half holding the lower half shut. There was a latch as well as the chain, but the chain was rather loose and when Grant raised the latch he was able to push the door open an inch or two before the chain drew tight and held it, leaving a small gap on the left-hand side. He pulled the torch out of his pocket, switched it on and shone the beam through the gap. He could not see a great deal, but what he did see was enough to convince him that his suspicions had been justified. The woman named Moira had told him that they did not run a car, but there was certainly one in the stable.

He could see no more than part of the rear end of the car, but from this he was able to satisfy himself on at least two points: it was a sports model and it was red. If he had been invited to do so he would have been prepared to lay a small bet that it was also an MGB.

He switched off the torch and put it back in his pocket, and the dog was really making a hell of a racket now. So he pulled the door shut and he was just turning away from the stable when he heard a man's voice.

'Don't move,' the man said, 'or I'll blast your guts out.'

Grant stopped his turn half-way, but he completed the turning of his head and saw, as he had feared, that the man was carrying a shotgun and that the gun was pointed at that area of the body which he had threatened to blast. The moonlight was on him and Grant could see that he was a tall, rather skinny man with a lot of wild-looking hair and a beard. He was dressed in shorts and a shirt, with a pair of gumboots on his feet, having probably donned these clothes in haste when he heard the dog barking. The gun in his hands appeared to be a single-barrelled twelve-bore.

'Do you mind not pointing that thing at me?' Grant said. 'It might go off.'

'You bet it might,' the man said. 'What in hell do you think you're doing?'

'Just looking round.'

'Looking round! Do you know what time it is?'

'Yes,' Grant said.

There were some lights showing in the house and two or three more people had come out and were walking towards the stables. Grant could see the woman named Moira wrapped in a dressing-gown. There was no sign of the blonde woman. As soon as she got closer Moira recognised him.

'That's the man who was here earlier. The one I told you about.'

Grant completed his turn. He felt reasonably sure the man with the gun was not going to shoot him.

'Yes,' he said, 'I was here this morning.'

'Why did you come back?' the man demanded.

'I wanted to make sure about the car.'

'What car?' Moira said.

Grant gave a jerk of the thumb in the direction of the stable behind him. 'The one in there. A red MGB. Like the one I asked about this morning and you said you'd never seen. Remember?'

The woman said nothing.

'What business is it of yours?' the man with the gun demanded.

'Would you like to tell me who the car belongs to?'

There were three other men and a

couple more women there now, but still not the blonde and none of the children. Grant could sense the hostility; he would have had to be particularly insensitive not to have done so. They had a common dislike, and it was of him.

'Why should I?' the man said.

'Because a woman the police are looking for owns a car like that.'

'Why should we help the police?'

'I'm not asking you to. But if you help me you could be helping her.'

'So you still think we've got somebody named Melissa Lloyd staying here?' Moira said.

'I'm sure you have.'

'You'd better be on your way,' the man with the gun said. 'You're not welcome here.'

'I already had that impression.'

'So why don't you beat it before the gun goes off — accidentally.'

'You wouldn't let that happen,' Grant said. But he was not so sure; he had a feeling that the man might be just a shade crazy, and a crazy man pointing a shotgun at your stomach was not to be trifled with. Maybe it was time to be on his way.

'You really had better go,' Moira said. She seemed anxious. Perhaps she was not sure what the man might do. 'There's nothing for you here.'

'All right,' Grant said, 'I'll go. But I think you're being rather foolish.'

He was not very happy about turning his back on the man with the shotgun, but it would have been ridiculous to walk away backwards. So he turned and his flesh crawled a bit as he went, not hurrying it, controlling the urge to run, to get out of range as quickly as possible. He was half expecting to hear the report of the gun, but there was nothing; no sound but the barking of the dog and the restless stamping of the horse. So maybe the man was not so crazy after all; maybe there was not even a cartridge in the gun. But that was a chance it was never safe to bank on; you could get yourself a bellyful of lead pellets acting on that kind of assumption.

When he came to the pond he turned his head and he could see them all standing there, an amorphous group in the cold moonlight, not moving, watching him to make sure that he really left the place. He was going to do that; they had no need to fear he would not; he had got the answer to his question and there was nothing more he could do there — not without co-operation; and he was dead sure he was not going to get any of that, not from the commune.

He walked back up the lane and came to the place where he had left the Cortina. He got in and sat there, not switching on the lights or the ignition, just waiting. He knew that he could be wasting his time; it was just a hunch. But there were times when you had to act on hunches, and sometimes it worked out. This might be one of those times. And on the other hand it might not. So just have patience. Patience, Sam, patience.

Half an hour passed. It was darker now; there was a good deal of cloud about and a few drops of rain pattered on the windscreen. The air had become noticeably chilly, but Grant left the window down. The distant barking of the dog had died away and the only sound was the occasional hooting of an owl. Maybe he was wasting his time.

When he looked at his watch again he saw that it was getting on for a quarter to two; he must have been sitting there for at least an hour. He decided to wait until two o'clock and if nothing had happened by then he would pack it in, because it began to look as though he had had the wrong hunch.

Fifteen more minutes ticked by and he was feeling cold and stiff and depressed. Okay, he thought, this is it; this is where I sign off. He reached for the ignition key and as he did so he heard the sound of a car engine and caught the flash of headlights further down the lane. So it had been a good hunch after all; it had just taken a bit longer than he had expected, and he had almost missed the boat; another couple of minutes and he would have been away.

He got the engine going and took the Cortina out of the gateway and shunted it across the lane and stopped it there, blocking the way. Then he switched off the engine and waited for the other car.

There was a slight bend in the lane about thirty yards from where he had stopped, and the other car came round it at a steady pace, because it was not the kind of surface for speeding. The headlights picked up the Cortina and the driver of the other car stood on the brakes and brought it to a halt, and Grant could imagine the shock it must have been to spot another vehicle blocking the lane. But life was full of shocks and you just had to learn to take them. He had had plenty himself.

He got out of the Cortina and walked towards the other car with the headlights full on him, and he hoped the crazy young man was not sitting back there with the shotgun waiting for him. But he was pretty sure it was not the man, and he walked on out of the dazzle of the lights and saw that he had been right: it was a red MGB and there was just one person sitting in it — a woman.

The hood was up but the side window was open, and he looked in and said: 'I'm glad you came. It's been a long wait.'

She was not wearing the dark glasses

now, and the blonde hair was not fooling him either; you could dye your hair or you could wear a wig, and he would have put his money on the wig. There was not a lot of light inside the MGB and he could not have sworn that the face he was looking at matched the one in the photograph that Sanchez had given him, but he felt damned sure it did.

'What do you want?' she said. She was wearing a quilted anorak and dark slacks and a pair of string-back gloves.

'A talk.'

'I don't want to talk to you. I don't want to talk to anyone. Now will you please get that car out of my way.'

'After I've been to all this trouble to find you, Miss Lloyd? You can't really expect me to do that. And where are you going?'

'That's none of your damned business.' She sounded nervous, on edge. Grant could understand that.

'Looking for another hiding-place, another bolt-hole? Is that it? Afraid I'll bring the police on you down here?' It was what he had been counting on; it was why he had stayed. He had scared her into making a run for it. 'Have you anywhere to go?'

'I — ' she said; and then she seemed to crack up. Her hands were gripping the top of the steering-wheel and she just slumped forward, her head dropping on to the string-back gloves, and began to cry.

He had not expected her to do that; he would have imagined her to be tougher. But maybe she had been under strain for a long time, and maybe she was no tougher than the next person when you got down to the basics. There was a limit to what anyone could take.

'Now,' he said, 'there's no need for that. It's not the end of the world, you know.' He put a hand on her shoulder and he could feel her shaking. He felt sorry for her, but he told himself it might just be an act she was putting on to win his sympathy and he had better watch it. She would not have been the first one who had played him for a sucker.

'Look,' he said, 'this could be the best thing that could have happened — from your point of view. You couldn't have gone on hiding in that commune for the rest of your life; some day somebody would have been bound to find you. Maybe you were lucky I was the one.'

She had stopped crying. He took his hand away and she sat up. 'So what's so special about you? How are you any better than the rest?'

'Well, for one thing, I'm not the police. And for another, and more important thing, I'm not interested in shutting your mouth.'

He could tell by the little gasp she gave that she knew what he meant by that and that he had touched a nerve. She was scared sure enough; not so much of the police maybe, but certainly of some other people. She was silent for a while and he let her think about it. He guessed she was wondering just how far she could trust him; and possibly she was wanting to, wanting someone to lean on.

Finally she said: 'You talked this morning about being able to help me. How can you do that?'

It was rather a difficult question to

answer satisfactorily, because helping her really meant persuading her to go to the police and tell them all she knew; that was the only way she was going to get herself completely off the hook. But it was no use telling her that at the present moment, so he skated round it.

'Well, for a start I know a place where you can go until we get things sorted out. Somewhere safe.'

He caught the quick glance of her eyes and he felt pretty sure she had not had an idea where to go for refuge; she had just known that she had to get away from the commune because it was no longer safe for her there. He had flushed her out and got her on the run, but now he was offering her another sanctuary and she was listening. But she was still suspicious; she was bound to be.

'Where is this place you're talking of?'

'It's my flat in London. There's nobody there.' He thought of Susan Sims and it still made him wince to think that she had gone; but maybe there was some good in that ill wind, since he would never have been able to offer the flat as a refuge for

Miss Lloyd if Miss Sims had still been in residence.

'Are you suggesting we should go there right now?' The doubt was apparent in her voice; she was looking for the catch. And yet he felt that she wanted to be persuaded; it would solve the immediate problem, take the responsibility off her shoulders if only for the moment.

'Why not?' Grant said. 'We can't just stay here.'

'You haven't told me who you're working for.'

'It doesn't matter. Not the people you're afraid of; I can tell you that.'

'How can I be sure you're telling the truth? That you're who you say you are.'

'I can show you my driver's licence and I've got a card somewhere. Do you want to see them?'

'No,' she said. 'I'll take your word.'

'And you'll do what I've suggested?'

'What about this car? Where can we put it when we get there?'

'There's a lock-up garage I use. It'll be all right in there.'

She gave it some more consideration,

but it was obvious that she could think of nothing better, and in the end she gave a sigh of resignation and said: 'All right; I'll do it.'

'Good. Now you'd better hang on to my tail, but in case you lose me this is my address.' He gave it to her. 'How are you off for petrol?'

'A bit low.'

'We'll stop at the first all-night filling station we come to, then. Okay?'

'Okay.'

'And Melissa.'

'Yes, Sam?'

'Don't try to give me the slip. If you do that I shall just have to alert the police and they'll be on to you before you can bat an eyelid. They've been looking for you everywhere.'

'I know,' she said.

'Let's be on our way, then.'

He walked back to the Cortina and started it up and took it out of the lane and on to the tarred road. He could see the lights of the MGB in the driving mirror and he felt sure she would not try to give him the slip. She was alone and she needed someone and he was there; those were good reasons why she would hang on. After a time they got away from the minor roads and he spotted some lighted petrol pumps and pulled on to the forecourt of the garage. The MGB followed and he got out of the Cortina and walked back and had a word with her.

'You're feeling all right?'

'Yes,' she said, 'I'm all right.'

'Well, don't go to sleep at the wheel.'

'I've never felt less like sleeping.'

He could well believe that. Maybe he was the one who should take care not to fall asleep.

'You're not hungry?'

'No,' she said, 'I'm not hungry.'

When both tanks had been filled up they got under way again and every so often he would take a look in the mirror to make sure the MGB was hanging on; and it was. Miss Lloyd appeared to be a competent driver and he came to the conclusion that there was no need to worry about her; even if he lost her she would reach their destination without trouble. In fact he did lose her once or twice, but each time she caught up again and they were just about nose to tail when they got to the lock-up garage and stowed the MGB away. He was glad to have it off the road, because although the police were hardly likely to be keeping a very sharp look-out for it any longer, it was just possible that some officious copper with a cast-iron memory might remember that a red MGB was on the wanted list and might check on the number.

'You did that well,' he said.

She gave him a quick glance. It had been growing light as they came into London and he could see her more clearly now. Even at that hour in the morning with a damp chill in the air, even though she had lost a night's sleep and had just driven about a hundred miles, she still looked like somebody rather special. Once again, as when he had studied the photograph which Sanchez had given him, he felt he could understand why Olmedo should have taken up with her. She was younger than he had judged her to be when he had seen her wearing the dark glasses and with her hands covered in flour; he doubted now whether she was much more than twenty-five.

'What did I do well?'

'The driving.'

'Oh, that.' She seemed to dismiss it with a grimace. 'Where is this flat of yours?'

'Not far from here.'

'Are you taking your car?'

'Yes.'

She got in. She had a suitcase which had been in the boot of the MGB and she tossed it on to the rear seat. Grant turned the Cortina into the cul-de-sac and they did the last part of the journey in little more than a minute. He took his holdall out of the boot and locked the car and led the way up to the flat, which was really nothing more than a few rooms on the second floor of a big old house that had come down in the world. There was no sound of anyone stirring; nobody got up as early as that, not in that house. He found his key and unlocked the door and stood aside to let the girl go past. Then he followed her in and closed the door.

With the grey light of morning creeping into it, the flat presented a depressing aspect, and he wondered what kind of impression it was making on Melissa Lloyd. Maybe she had been expecting something more in the luxury class, more in the style of what Olmedo had provided. But then he reflected that she must be a girl who could take the rough with the smooth; there had certainly been very little in the way of luxury at the commune, and maybe none when she had been living with the porn photographer either, if it came to that.

'It's not much,' he said with a hint of apology. 'But it does for me.'

She had put the suitcase down and he wondered whether she was regretting having allowed herself to be persuaded into coming. But she had had little alternative; it had practically been forced on her.

'It's all right,' she said. Her voice sounded flat and colourless, rather tired.

He was wondering about the next

move. He had told her that he wanted to talk to her — and he still did. But they had both had a sleepless night and the best thing might be to get their heads down for a few hours and start on the talking when they were a bit fresher. But he did not immediately suggest it. Instead, he said. 'I think I'll make some coffee. Would you like some?'

'That seems like a good idea,' she said; but still with no suggestion of enthusiasm.

'Maybe I should lash up some breakfast as well.'

'You eat if you like,' she said, 'but just coffee for me. I'm not really hungry.'

'In that case I think we'll leave the food till later. Let me take your anorak; then you won't look so much as if you're just passing through.'

She gave the ghost of a smile at that. She pulled the zipper down and slipped out of the anorak. He took it from her, and he had just got it in his hand when the bedroom door opened and Susan Sims walked in. Miss Sims looked as if she had been wakened from a nice deep sleep and was none too pleased about it. Her hair was a bit tousled and she was wearing nothing but a short nylon nightdress and a pair of fur mules, and she came to a halt just inside the room and said.

'Well, thith ith nithe, I mutht thay.'

'Oh, Lord!' Grant said. 'I thought you'd left.'

Miss Sims looked at him and then she looked at Melissa Lloyd; and after that she looked at him again.

'Tho it would theem,' she said.

7

Hooked

'But I rang you,' Grant said. 'I rang four times and there was no answer.' Even though he was certainly glad to see she had not gone after all, he felt a little aggrieved. And of course it was going to be damned awkward. If only she had answered the phone.

'Tho what if you did ring?' Miss Sims said. 'Do you thuppothe I thtay in all the time you're away jutht waiting for you to call?'

'No, of course not. But you said you were leaving, so when I couldn't contact you I naturally supposed you had done just that.'

'And you couldn't even wait to make thertain. You thimply went out and picked up thomeone elthe.'

'No, I didn't. You've got it all wrong.'

'Oh, have I? Then who ith that

perthon?' She pointed an accusing finger at the other girl. 'Who ith that, may I athk?'

'This is Miss Lloyd,' Grant said.

Susan Sims appeared unconvinced. 'With blonde hair? That'th a likely thtory.'

'It's a wig,' Melissa said. She looked at Grant. 'You told me there would be nobody here.'

He felt as though he were being attacked from both sides. 'That's what I thought.'

'You didn't mention that you had a wife.'

'I haven't. This is Miss Susan Sims.'

'And she's living here?'

Miss Sims answered for herself. 'Of courthe I'm living here. Duthn't it look like it?'

'Yes, it does,' Melissa said; and she looked again at Grant. 'It's not going to work out, is it?'

'What ithn't?' Miss Sims demanded.

'He said I could stay here for a while.'

'Oh, he did, did he? And did he tell you there wath only one bedroom?'

'No, he didn't.'

Susan Sims glared at Grant. 'I might have known it. You damned Cathanova.'

'I think I'd better make the coffee,' Grant said.

He beat a hasty retreat to the kitchen and wondered how the devil he was going to sort this one out. He had so thoroughly convinced himself that Susan Sims had walked out on him that the possibility of her being in the flat had never for an instant entered his mind. Now things were really snagged up — unless she decided that the arrival of Melissa Lloyd was more than she could take and really did beat it. That would certainly solve the immediate problem, but not in a way he would have desired. He wanted her to stay; but if she stayed, what happened to Miss Lloyd? It was a mess, a fine old mess and no mistake.

He took his time over making the coffee, and when he went back into the other room he found Melissa there alone, sitting in one of the armchairs.

'She's getting dressed,' Melissa said, answering the unspoken question.

'She isn't packing, I suppose?'

'I couldn't say about that. You might have warned me, don't you think?'

'Warned you?'

'About what I might be walking into.'

'It didn't occur to me,' Grant said. He set the coffee tray down on the table. 'Help yourself, will you? I think I'd better go and see what's happening.'

He tapped on the bedroom door, walked in and closed the door behind him. Susan Sims had got herself into a pair of pale blue slacks and was pulling on a yellow jumper. There were some other items of clothing scattered about the room but no sign of any packing in progress, so it looked as though he had been wrong in thinking she might have decided to go. For the moment anyway.

'Ith that thtripper thtill here?' she demanded.

'Of course she's still here,' Grant said. 'She hasn't got anywhere else to go.'

'There mutht be plenty of platheth.'

'Well, maybe. But just for the present I want her where I can keep an eye on her.'

'I'll bet you do.'

'And not for the reason you seem to be

implying. I want to get her story.'

'What story?'

'About what happened that night when Mr Olmedo was murdered. She's the only witness. That's if she really did see it all.'

Miss Sims thought about it, and Grant was relieved to see that she appeared to be calming down. 'Ith that the only reathon you brought her here?'

'Yes. Don't you believe me?'

She thought about that too. Then she said: 'All right, I believe you, Tham.' And she gave him a kiss to prove it. 'But now you've found her I think you should go thraight to the polithe.'

'Not until I know what it's all about. She's frightened and I think she needs help.'

Miss Sims appeared to have some doubt about that; but all she said was: 'Aren't you going to let Mr Thancheth know you've found her?'

'All in good time. Nothing's going to be lost by keeping the ace up my sleeve for a while.'

'Well, if you think tho; but I thtill thay

it'th dangerouth to get micthed up in murder.'

'Don't let that worry you,' Grant said. 'I'm not really mixed up in it. And now let's have some coffee and hear what the lady has to say for herself.'

Melissa Lloyd, once she got going, had quite a lot to say for herself, and by the time she had finished Susan Sims was completely won over to her side and was making all kinds of sympathetic noises. Grant was a little more reserved in his judgement, and though he would not have gone so far as to say that the girl was lying, he had a feeling that she might be giving a strictly edited version of what had occurred on the fatal night; that in fact she was leaving bits out. He might be wrong, but that was the impression he got; and he wondered why. What was she hiding? What could she have to hide?

The story, even as she told it, was horrifying enough and provided good reason for her running away and staying in hiding. Many other people might have felt inclined to do precisely the same if caught in a similar situation.

'You know I was living with Enrique, of course?'

'With Mr Olmedo? Yes,' Grant said.

'Well, of course, you would. It was no secret. Especially after what happened. I suppose just about everybody in the country knew it.'

She was referring to the newspapers, Grant supposed. They had certainly made a splash with all the details they could dig up on the subject of Olmedo's love life; it was the kind of thing the popular Press revelled in — and its readers.

'They made it sound so — well — sordid. And it wasn't, you know. He was really in love with me.'

'And were you in love with him?'

She answered the question frankly. 'No. But I liked him. He was fun to be with. And he treated me with respect; it's not everyone who's done that. And another thing, he made me feel secure. I'd never had security before.'

'It didn't turn out to be very good security,' Grant said. 'Not exactly the lasting kind.'

'No.' She sounded wistful, perhaps

regretting that lost security. 'No, it didn't. But while it lasted I was happy. I don't think I've ever been so happy.'

'Not even at the commune? The first time, I mean.'

'Well,' she said; and there was a pensive look in her eyes, as though she were gazing back into the past and trying to remember just what it had been like, 'that was different. I suppose you might say I had contentment there. I liked it, but it was not the same as being with Enrique.'

Grant could believe that.

Miss Sims drank some coffeee and said: 'I think everybody hath a right to be happy.'

Melissa glanced at her and Grant saw her lips tremble. A few more minutes and the girls would be exchanging reminiscences and deep thoughts on the meaning of life. Which was not something he had on his agenda.

'How long had you been down at the Old Hall? That time, I mean.'

The question brought Melissa back to the subject. 'Oh, just a day or two. We'd gone down on the Wednesday; we were going to stay there over the weekend and then come back to London. Enrique had some business to attend to.'

'You travelled down together?'

'Yes. I drove him in the MGB. He hardly ever drove himself; he didn't like the traffic.'

'Did anything happen on the Thursday? Anything out of the ordinary, that is.'

'No. Enrique had a few phone calls, but that was not unusual.'

'He didn't seem at all worried?'

'I wouldn't have said so.'

'Did he tell you what the phone calls were about?'

'No; but he never talked to me about his business. That was one thing that was never mentioned. He said that when he was with me he liked to relax, forget about it.'

'So you have no idea who was calling him?'

'No.'

'And you're quite sure he didn't seem worried? After one particular call, perhaps.'

'No. He seemed happy; like a man who

everything is going right for. He didn't look as if he had a care in the world.'

'Did anybody come to the house? Any visitors?'

'Nobody. There was Mrs Jenner, of course, but no social callers. We weren't ever really accepted in the village, you know. Enrique didn't have any friends there or in the county.'

'So nothing on Thursday. What about Friday?'

'The same, more or less. Nothing unusual. Not until the night — '

They were coming to it now, Grant thought; and he wondered whether she had ever spoken about it to anyone else, to anyone in the commune. Perhaps, and perhaps not. Maybe she had kept it to herself, locked away in her memory. Perhaps now it would be a relief for her to share the secret — and the burden.

'Tell us what happened,' Grant said gently.

She took a deep breath, like a swimmer getting ready to dive, and then let it out again in an audible sigh. 'It was about one o'clock in the morning. We had gone to bed a little before midnight after watching a film on television. There was this banging on the front door — '

'Banging?'

'Well, knocking. I suppose they'd rung the bell, but neither of us had heard it, and then they started knocking. That's what woke us up. Enrique switched on the bedside lamp and looked at the clock, and then he said: 'My God! You see what time it is! Who's making all that racket at this hour?' And then he got out of bed and started putting on a dressing-gown. I said to him: 'Are you going down to open the door?' Because, I don't know why, but I was afraid. That knocking in the middle of the night, it scared me.'

'But he wasn't afraid?'

'No. He just said: 'I don't know anybody else who'll do it if I don't. Unless you'd like to.' I said: 'But, Enrique, you don't know who it is.' He laughed then and said: 'That is what I am going down to find out.' And then he picked up his gun and went down.'

'His gun?'

'He always kept one on the bedside table.'

'What kind of gun?'

'I don't know anything about those things. It was a small one, kind of squarish, black.'

It sounded like an automatic; but Walden had said nothing about a pistol. So maybe by the time the police arrived on the scene it had gone. Maybe somebody had decided it was untidy leaving it lying around; though they had not bothered much about tidiness in general, judging by what Mrs Jenner had said.

'So he went down to open the door. And what did you do?'

'I got out of bed and put a dressing-gown on. I was worried. I mean, people don't usually come knocking at the door at one o'clock in the morning. So I went out of the bedroom to see what was happening, and when I got to the head of the staircase there were these men walking into the hall.'

'How many men?'

'Two. One was wearing a black leather

car-coat and the other was in a blue trench-coat.'

'Did they see you?'

'No. I drew back at once and they didn't look up.'

'What was Olmedo doing?'

'He was leading the way, walking ahead of them.'

'To the drawing room?'

'Yes.'

'Was he going willingly?'

'I don't think so.'

'Why don't you think so?'

'He hadn't got the gun in his hand. The man in the leather coat had a gun. I couldn't see whether the other man had.'

'But there'd been no shooting?'

'No.'

'Do you think they jumped him when he opened the door, before he could use the gun?'

'It's possible. But it must have happened before I got to the stairs.'

'It may be, of course, that he recognised the men; that he'd had dealings with them, perhaps as business associates. In which case he might have been taken off guard, not realising what their purpose was until it was too late. Do you think that's how it could have been?'

'It could have, I suppose. I don't know.'

'You didn't recognise them?'

'No. But I never met his business associates. Like I told you, he kept all that away from me.'

'So then?'

'Then they all went into the drawing-room and closed the door.'

'Then what did you do?'

'I tiptoed downstairs and listened at the door.'

'Could you hear anything?'

'I could hear them moving about and there was a sound of voices, but I couldn't catch the words. Then I heard Enrique cry out: 'No!' It was very loud, almost a scream. And then again: 'No, no, no!' After that there was some more moving around and Enrique was protesting loudly. At least, that's what it seemed like.'

'That would be when they were tying him up?'

'I expect so.'

'You didn't feel like going in and helping him?' Grant said.

She looked at him as if he might have been suggesting she should take a dose of strychnine. 'What could I have done?'

Even Susan Sims appeared to think he was being unreasonable. 'There were two men, for goodneth thake. With a pithtol and a knife.'

He looked at Miss Lloyd. 'But you didn't know about the knife then?'

'No, but — '

'Well, it was just a thought.' He saw that it would have been rather a lot to expect her to do anything as impetuous as bursting into the room and trying to rescue Olmedo from his assailants. She had admitted that she had never been in love with him. 'You couldn't see anything, of course?'

'No. I tried to peep through the keyhole, but there was a key in the other side and it was no use. And then I heard one of the men say: 'We'd better take a look round.' I guessed he meant to take a look round the house to see if there was anyone else there, and I could only think of one thing then — to run away and hide. I was in a panic and I ran back upstairs and hid.'

'Where?'

'In a box-room on the top floor. In an old trunk.'

'And nobody found you?'

'No. I don't think they wasted much time looking. They must have been keen to go back and get to work on poor Enrique.'

'How long did you stay in the trunk?'

'About half an hour, I think, but I couldn't be sure exactly. Then I heard the sound of a car starting up and driving away, and I went downstairs and found Enrique.'

'It must have been a shock.'

'Yes,' she said, her lips trembling again, 'it was.'

'Why do you think they tortured him?'

'To make him tell them something, I suppose.'

'You don't know what it was?'

'No.'

'Why did you run away?'

'Because I was afraid.'

'What were you afraid of? The men had gone.'

'I don't know. I was just terrified, that's all. I thought they would get me and I couldn't think of anything else to do but get away from there. And then I thought of the commune and it seemed the only place to go.'

'You didn't think of going to the police?'

'You've got to believe me,' she said, 'when I tell you it just didn't come into my head. I simply panicked and that's all there is to it. Don't you understand?'

'I understand,' Susan Sims assured her; and she gave Miss Lloyd's hand a squeeze. 'I'd have done exactly the thame in your plathe.'

Well, it might be the truth, Grant thought; but he had his doubts about whether it was the whole truth and nothing but the truth. There was something about the feel of it that was not quite right, though he could not have said precisely what.

'So that's it?' he said.

'That's it.'

'And you've been living in the commune ever since?'

'Yes.'

'You've got some very good friends there.'

'Yes, I have.'

'Who was the one with the shotgun?'

'That was Pete. After you'd gone he tried to persuade me not to leave. He said he'd protect me.'

'Is he in love with you?' Grant asked.

'I think he thinks he is.'

'What ith all thith about a gun?' Susan Sims asked.

Grant told her.

'Tho I wath right,' she said. 'I warned you that you could get yourthelf killed.'

'But I didn't get myself killed.'

'There'th thtill time,' Miss Sims said darkly.

'So even after you'd had time to get over your panic,' Grant said to Melissa, 'you still didn't think it might be a good idea to tell the police all about what happened down at the Old Hall that night?'

'I was still afraid of those men. I still

am. They must know I was in the house when they killed Enrique; it was in the papers. So don't you think they'll be wanting to get rid of me? To make sure I never get the chance to identify them.'

'It's possible,' Grant admitted.

'You know it's more than possible. You said as much when you were urging me to come here with you. You said I'd be safe here. Have you forgotten?'

'No, I haven't forgotten. Only it's not quite so simple now, is it?' He glanced at Susan Sims.

'It'th perfectly thimple,' Miss Sims said. 'Melitha can thleep in my bed and you can thleep in here on the thofa.'

'Well, thanks very much,' Grant said. But he was quite happy about it. It was the arrangement he would have suggested himself, but it was better that she should have done so; it avoided any argument. And it would not be for long.

He questioned Miss Lloyd again. 'What information do you think those men were trying to get out of Mr Olmedo?'

'I don't know,' she said. 'I just don't know.'

'Nothing he had said would give you any clue? Some chance remark perhaps.'

'No, nothing.'

'And you say you'd never seen the men before?'

'No.'

'It seems likely they were looking for something; they made a search of the house. So no doubt they were trying to make him tell them where it was hidden. Had he ever mentioned anything? Something of value.'

She shook her head. 'He never spoke of anything of that sort to me.'

'Or of any important papers, documents, that kind of thing?'

'I told you he never mentioned business to me.'

Grant saw that he was not going to get anything more from her. Yet there must have been something of value in the house, of more than ordinary value; he felt sure of it. If the men had merely wished to kill Olmedo they would have done it quickly and got away; hired killers would not have played around with the victim. And the killing itself seemed almost like an afterthought, unpremeditated perhaps. But it was all conjecture; and why should he bother his head about it anyway? He had found the lady, and that was all Sanchez had asked him to do. So why not leave it at that? Well, maybe because the thing had got him hooked. It was like a drug and it really had him hooked.

'What are you going to do, Tham?' Susan Sims asked.

He stood up and yawned. 'I'm going to have a shave and then catch a wink or two of sleep. I'm fagged out.' He turned to Melissa. 'And I suggest you do the same — omitting the shave, of course. After that we'll have to think of something.'

8

The Way it Really Was

He slept on the sofa and woke a couple of hours later with a stiff neck and a dry mouth. He stood up and stretched himself and saw that there was a note from Miss Sims propped up on the table. It read: 'Have gone shopping. Back soon. Love S.'

He massaged his neck and went into the kitchen and made a pot of tea and washed the dryness out of his mouth. He was feeling hungry and he ate some breakfast biscuits to take the edge off his appetite; and then he peeped into the bedroom and saw that Melissa Lloyd was asleep in the bed. The curtains were still drawn and the room was in a kind of twilight, but he could see her handbag on the dressing-table. He walked over and opened it, and she was still sleeping like a child. She had taken off the blonde wig and he thought she looked even better with her natural hair, though it could maybe have used some attention from a hairdresser.

There was the usual junk in the handbag, but he was not interested in anything but the keys. He took them out and slipped them into his pocket. Then he refastened the handbag and left the bedroom, closing the door softly behind him. Miss Lloyd had not even stirred.

The Cortina was still parked outside the house, but he left it there and walked to the lock-up garage. It was a dull morning and there was a threat of rain, but none falling. There was a man backing a brand-new Datsun out of the garage next to his and being very careful not to scratch the paint. Grant was on nodding terms with him and he got the nod before the man drove off in his bright new piece of Japanese engineering, not giving a damn whether British Leyland went down the drain or not.

Grant unlocked his garage and looked at the MGB and thought what a nice little car it was and what a nice little present it had been from the late Mr Enrique Olmedo to his one-time stripper girlfriend. Too bad he was no longer around to enjoy Miss Lloyd's gratitude and her undoubted physical charms. But that was life — or rather, death — and you had to take what was offered while you had the chance, because it was a dead cert you could never count on any jam tomorrow.

Still, philosophising was not going to get him anywhere, and he had not walked to the garage simply to stand there and admire Miss Lloyd's car, so he took the keys he had filched from her handbag out of his pocket and opened the boot.

The first thing he saw was the parcel. He could hardly have missed seeing it, because it was a big, square-sided package wrapped in brown paper and fastened with sticky tape. He lifted it out and was surprised to find how heavy it was; about twenty-five pounds or more, he would have said. He set it carefully down on the floor of the garage and took another look inside the boot, but there was nothing else of interest and there was nothing in the front of the car to cause any excitement, either. He relocked the boot, picked up the parcel, closed and locked the garage, and walked back to the flat.

There were a couple of middle-aged women coming down the stairs as he went up. They had a flat on the first floor and he gave them a nod, and one of them said she thought it would turn to rain and the other one looked at his parcel with suspicion, as though she suspected it might be a bomb. And for all he knew, it might have been at that. He said he thought it would rain, too, and went on up the stairs.

He let himself into the flat and stood the parcel on the table in the sitting room. There was not a sound coming from the bedroom, so he guessed Miss Lloyd was still catching up on her sleep. He fetched a knife from the kitchen and proceeded to cut the paper off the parcel. He knew it was not the sort of thing he had any legal right to do, and he knew that Miss Lloyd would have every justification for feeling very much disgruntled when she found out that he had taken such a liberty with her property; or at least what was presumably her property; but he did it nevertheless.

When he had got the paper stripped off he came to a stout cardboard box, and inside the box was a statuette or figurine, apparently made of pottery. He was not very well versed in such things, but he would have hazarded a guess that it had originated in South America and represented an Inca monarch or something of the sort. Whether or not it was of any great value he had no idea; but he would have been ready to stake a few new pence that Melissa Lloyd believed it was, and with a bit of persuasion he might even have jacked the stake up to a few pounds.

'Well, well, well,' he muttered. 'So the lovely lady wasn't telling the truth, the whole truth and nothing but the truth. Who can you trust?'

He thought the matter over and he wondered whether Sanchez knew about the statuette. But there seemed to be no reason why he should; it was very likely something that his cousin had acquired privately. If Sanchez had had any knowledge of it, he would certainly have reported its loss to the police; but he had not done so. And then Grant remembered that Mrs Jenner had not mentioned it either; so it looked as though Olmedo — always supposing it had been his — had kept it hidden away, since it was far too conspicuous an object for the housekeeper to have over-looked when she had been checking whether anything had been stolen. So what now? What now, Sammy?

He began to gather up the brown paper, and he was folding it into a neat pile when he heard the bedroom door open. He turned and looked at her, shaking his head slightly in admonishment.

'You didn't tell us the truth, did you? You didn't tell it exactly as it happened.'

She was wearing a plain blue pyjama suit and the sleep was still in her eyes. But there was not enough of it to prevent her seeing what it was that was standing on the table.

'You had no right,' she said.

'Maybe not. But I did it just the same.'

'It was a low, mean, sneaking thing to do.'

'I do sometimes do low, mean, sneaking things,' Grant said. 'It's part of the job, I'm afraid. Much of the time it's a low, mean, sneaking kind of a job.'

'You took the keys out of my handbag while I was asleep.'

'Yes, I did that too.'

'I suppose you're proud of yourself.'

'I wouldn't say that. Pride doesn't really come into it. I simply looked for something and found it. Unlike some other people we both know about.'

'So now that you've found it, what do you propose to do?' He could sense that she was uneasy, but she was defiant too.

'I propose to listen patiently while you give me a more accurate account of what happened on the night of the murder. Particularly as regards your own actions. Do you want to get dressed first? I can make some more coffee while you're about it. Coffee seems to be good for confessions.'

If there had been anything close at hand he believed she would have thrown it at him; but there was nothing, and all she did was clench her fists and glare at him. And then she turned abruptly and went back into the bedroom and slammed the door. He took that as meaning that she was going to dress, and he went into the kitchen to make coffee for the second time that morning. Add in the pot of tea, and he was really keeping busy in the brewing-up line. When he took the coffee into the sitting room she was already there, fully dressed and with the blonde wig in place again. He put the coffee on the table beside the statuette.

'So you've decided to tell it the way it was?'

She made no answer to the question; she just looked at him with a lot of dislike. At least it was not a direct refusal, or even a denial that the record needed putting straight, so he poured the coffee and handed her a cup, and after she had taken a mouthful or two she began to talk.

'All right,' she said, 'so it wasn't quite the way I told it.'

'I had an idea it wasn't even when you

were giving us the story. There seemed to be a few false notes here and there.'

She gave a sigh; her anger seemed to have evaporated and she was just dispirited. 'I knew you didn't believe it all. Maybe I'm a bad liar.'

'Not too bad at that,' Grant said.

She smiled faintly. 'Do I take that as a compliment?' She drank some more coffee and set the cup down. 'Anyway,' she said, 'it did start the way I told it. I saw the men come in and I saw Enrique go with them to the drawing room.'

'And then?'

'Then I suddenly thought I knew what they'd come for; it was like a sort of flash of intuition. I lied when I told you Enrique had never spoken to me about anything of value in the house. He had shown me that.' She pointed at the statuette.

'And he said it was valuable?'

'He said it was the most valuable single article he possessed. He said it was worth a fortune.'

'It doesn't look worth such a lot,' Grant said.

'No, it doesn't, does it? That's exactly what I told him, and he said it showed how little I knew about objects of that kind. Which was true enough; I don't know the first thing about them.'

'I don't either.'

'No? Well, you'll just have to take my word.'

'Like you took his?'

'Oh, he wouldn't lie to me. Why should he? If he said it was valuable you can be sure it is.'

'Where did he keep it?'

'Now that's the funny thing — well, not funny really, but you know what I mean. He kept it in that cardboard box under the bed. He said nobody would ever think of looking there and it was safer than it would have been stowed away under lock and key.'

'But you didn't agree, did you? You thought those men would find it.'

'Yes, I did. I didn't put any faith in hiding things under beds; so when I'd seen them marching Enrique off to the drawing room at gun-point I went back and grabbed it.'

'Then what did you do?'

'I took it up on to the roof.'

'The roof?' That was something he had not been expecting.

'Yes. It's flat and I'd been up there before; you get a marvellous view. There's a ladder leading to a doorway by one of the chimney-stacks, like a sort of companion-way on a boat; so, as I said, I carried the box up there and shut the door.'

'And they didn't search the roof?'

'One of them did, but he'd only got one of those little pencil torches and I moved round to keep the chimneys between us, and after a few minutes I heard the other one shouting to him to come down, and he went. I was half-frozen, because it was a cold night, and I was scared too, scared sick; and after he'd gone I just crouched down, trying to get out of the wind, and shivered.'

'Did you have any idea of what they were doing to Mr Olmedo?'

'No. How could I?'

'You must have guessed they wouldn't

be handling him very gently.'

'Well, what could I do?'

'You could have gone down and telephoned the police.'

'But suppose they had heard me?'

'They were pretty fully occupied, weren't they? You could have used the bedroom extension.'

'There isn't one. Enrique wouldn't have one put in. He said if anybody wanted to call him when he was down there they could do it in the daytime. Anyway, I was too terrified to move.'

It might have been the truth, but she had not been too terrified to think about the statuette and move it to a safer place. So maybe she thought the men were going to kill Olmedo and it might be a good idea to make sure of her own financial future by grabbing the most valuable thing in sight. Or would that be to judge her too harshly?

'He must have told them where it was eventually.'

'Why do you say that?' she asked, giving him a quick, searching glance.

'It seems likely. No man can hold out

under that kind of torture for long. I'd say he very soon told them to look under the bed, and when they found nothing there they came down and carved him up a bit more. But of course he couldn't tell them where it really was because he didn't know. And maybe he didn't say a word about you, seeing how much he loved you. In the end they got so mad at him they just lost control and stuck the knife in deep. Or at least one of them did. And then they searched the place and beat it.'

'What you're saying is that I'm responsible for his death. That's what you mean, isn't it?'

'No. You couldn't have foreseen what would happen. And maybe they would have killed him anyway.'

'But you don't believe that.'

'It doesn't matter what I believe. It's all done and we can't alter it. Did you wait on the roof until they'd gone?'

'Yes, the rest of it is just like I told you. I heard the car drive away and I went down and found him. It was horrible. I went to the bathroom and was sick. And I knew I had to get away from there; I couldn't bear to be in the house with him the way he was after they'd done with him.'

Yet she had had sufficient presence of mind, he reflected, to pack her things. According to Mrs Jenner she had left nothing. And she had not omitted to take the statuette, either; she had even found time to wrap it in brown paper first. He doubted whether she had told anyone at the commune about that; it had probably remained safely stowed away in the boot of the MGB all the time she was there. And of course that would explain why she would not have wanted to get into a tangle with the police. Police could ask so many damned awkward questions.

'What did you intend to do with this?' He tapped the statuette with his finger.

'I don't know. When I took it up to the roof it was to save it for Enrique. Maybe you don't believe me, but it was. But then he was dead, and I thought how he would never give me anything else and I knew he would have wanted me to have something; and so I took it.'

'You might have had difficulty in selling it.'

'I didn't even think about that.'

Again she might have been speaking the truth. It was hard to be sure. He thought about Sanchez again and wondered whether this was the time to tell her about him. She had not mentioned his name, so maybe Olmedo had never told her he had a cousin who was a partner in the business. But before he could get going on that subject Susan Sims walked in with a load of groceries.

She spotted the statuette at once. 'Where on earth did that come from?'

Grant looked at Melissa.

'You tell her,' she said. 'Tell it all.'

Grant told it all. Susan Sims listened without saying a word until he had finished. Then she looked at Melissa and said:

'He wath fooling you.'

Melissa seemed startled. 'Who was?'

'Mr Olmedo.'

'What do you mean? How was he fooling me?'

'About that thing.' Miss Sims pointed

at the Inca statuette. 'It ithn't valuable, you know. That'th all poppy-cock.'

'Now look,' Grant said, 'what do you know about South American art treasures.'

'Ith that what it'th thuppothed to be?'

'Well, of course it is. Why else would it be valuable?'

'But it ithn't. I jutht told you, didn't I?'

'So you know better than Mr Olmedo? He said it was the most valuable thing in his possession.'

'And that'th why I thay he wath fooling Melitha.'

'He wouldn't have done that,' Melissa said. 'I'm sure he wouldn't.'

'He mutht have done if he told you that thing wath valuable.'

'How can you be so sure it isn't?'

'Becauthe I know a thop in the Wetht End where you can buy ath many ath you want jutht like it at twenty-five poundth a time.'

'Now who's doing the fooling?' Grant said.

'Not me. I'm telling the thimple truth.'

'Twenty-five pounds,' Melissa said. 'Are you sure?'

'You bet I'm thure.'

'Maybe they're not really like this,' Grant said. 'Maybe they're just copies.'

'They look like it.'

'Reproductions usually do look like the original. That's the point.'

'Well, what'th to prove thith ith the original? More likely it'th jutht one of the crowd.'

She might well have something there, he thought. All they had to prove the statuette was a genuine collector's piece was what Melissa Lloyd said Olmedo had said. Olmedo might have been joking, having a game with her; and that could include the business of keeping it under the bed. Yet if that were so, why would the men have gone to such lengths to make him tell where it was hidden? But of course there was no proof that they had tortured him for that purpose; it was all a surmise. So maybe it would not be a bad idea to do a bit of checking up.

He spoke to Susan Sims. 'Do you think you could take me to the shop where they sell the statuettes?'

'Whenever you like. It'th in the Thtrand.'

'Right, then. We'll have an early lunch and we'll go there.'

'Do you propose taking me with you?' Melissa asked.

'Do you want to come?'

'Not particularly.'

'Can I trust you not to run off as soon as my back is turned?'

'Why should I run off?' she asked. 'I've nowhere to go. This is my bolt-hole now.'

There was some logic in that. And she would not be able to take the MGB because he still had her keys, not to mention the key to the garage. So it would probably be safe enough to leave her. He would look a fool, of course, if after going to so much trouble to find her he lost her again without even giving Sanchez a chance to speak to her; but it was not much of a risk. Besides, he was beginning to think there was a lot more to this business than he had at first supposed. He was getting some more hunches, and he was hooked all right; he really was hooked.

'Okay,' he said, 'you stay here. Maybe you could catch up on some more of that lost beauty sleep.'

'Maybe I could,' she said.

Not that she needed any beauty sleep as far as he could see.

9

Another of the Same

The shop in the Strand sold curios and copper trays and pottery and glassware and a thousand and one other things. There was nothing in it of any great value, but of what there was there was a considerable quantity and the turnover was probably large. The Inca statuettes were there in force, a row of them on a shelf like soldiers on parade, and all the dead spit of the one they had left in the flat with Miss Lloyd to keep it company.

Susan Sims pointed a finger at them in triumph. 'There you thee! What did I tell you! Now do you believe me?'

'I never disbelieved you,' Grant said.

'You can thay that now, but I'll bet you didn't think they'd be here.'

'You're quite mistaken. I should have been very disappointed if they hadn't been.'

She looked at him in slight puzzlement, as though not sure whether he was serious or not. 'You would?'

'Certainly I should,' Grant assured her. 'Let's take a closer look at them.'

They walked over to the shelf and he lifted one of the statuettes in his hands. It felt about the same weight as the one in the flat. A salesman approached as he was putting it down, a rather weedy man with a hollow chest and a forward thrust of his head like a hen searching for grains of corn. He was wearing a dark suit and thick-rimmed glasses; his voice was carefully modulated, polite but not obsequious.

'May I assist you, sir?'

'I was feeling the weight of this statuette. It's pretty heavy.'

'Yes indeed, sir. Quite a weight. Not easily knocked over. That could be an advantage.'

'South American, isn't it?'

'Peruvian. A representation of one of the old Inca rulers who were overthrown by the Spanish conquistadors.' He seemed to have been polishing up his

New World history. Maybe he had borrowed a copy of Prescott from the public library.

'But not antique?'

The man smiled. 'With a row of identical models to choose from at twenty-five pounds apiece! I'm afraid that would be a little too much to expect, sir.'

'But would there be an original from which these were copied? The way you get reproductions of old master paintings.'

'That I couldn't tell you, sir. The statuettes are supplied to us in quantity. I'm afraid I haven't made a deep study of Inca art and really have no idea whether there were such objects as this in pre-Spanish times.'

Grant nodded. 'I understand. It was just an idea. If I buy one it would be rather nice to know it's a genuine reproduction of something the Incas themselves actually had in their houses. Don't you agree?'

'Oh, entirely.' The suggestion that Grant was seriously thinking of buying one of the statuettes seemed to have revived the salesman's interest, which had shown signs of flagging. 'Of course, I can't positively guarantee it, but I would certainly think it most probable.'

'They do in fact come from Peru? They're not made in Stoke-on-Trent or somewhere like that?'

'Oh, no; I can assure you of that.' The man was quite eager now. It appeared to be rather quiet in the shop and he had no other customers clamouring for attention. 'Indeed, if you wish I can show you the invoice of a consignment we had in only yesterday. There's a fairly brisk demand for this particular line at the moment.'

'That would be very obliging of you,' Grant said.

'No trouble at all, sir. Only too happy to be of service.'

The salesman glided away as if he were moving on roller-skates. Susan Sims looked at Grant in some surprise.

'You don't really intend buying one of thothe thingth?'

'Why not? I can shove it down on the expense account.'

'You mutht be crathy. What on earth do you want one for?'

'Comparison.'

'You thtill don't believe they're the thame ath the other one?'

'I'd like to make sure.'

She shrugged. 'Okay, it'th your money.'

'Mr Peking's money,' Grant said.

The salesman came back with a sheet of paper in his hand. He showed it to Grant. It was an invoice for fifty Inca statuettes and it was headed. 'Olsan-Peru Import-Export Company.'

'Not from Stoke-on-Trent, you see,' the salesman remarked. He kept his thumb carefully over the part where the price was written in, not wishing to reveal to the customer just how much the mark-up was.

'Well,' Grant said, 'that seems pretty convincing. They would hardly be likely to send them all the way to South America just to bring them back again.'

The salesman smiled indulgently. 'No, sir, they wouldn't, would they?'

Grant bought one of the statuettes and took a receipt to show Mr Peking when he put in a claim for the cost of it on his expense account. He was not at all sure he would get it allowed, because strictly speaking this was not at all what he had been engaged to do; it was by way of being a private private investigation, and if Peking had known about it he would almost certainly have disapproved. So perhaps it was just as well he did not know.

The statuette was packed in a card-board box very similar to that from which he had taken the other one. The salesman handed it to him and expressed the hope that they would do further business together at some unspecified future date. Grant doubted it, but refrained from saying so. Let the man have his dreams.

Outside the shop he turned left, walking in the direction of Charing Cross station. Susan Sims stayed close by his side, dodging the other pedestrians.

'Well,' she said, 'I hope you're thatith-fied. Are we going home now?'

'After I've made a phone call.'

'Why don't you wait until you get back to the flat?'

'Because I want to do it now.'

'Okay,' she said. 'Pleathe yourthelf.'

He made the call from a box at Charing Cross station. He got through to Scotland Yard and asked to speak to Detective Sergeant Walden. He was lucky; Walden had just come in, but he sounded none too pleased.

'So it's you again. What do you want this time?'

'To ask a question.'

'You can ask,' Walden said; but the way he said it seemed to imply that there was no guarantee of an answer.

'That firm you were telling me Olmedo had an interest in — it wouldn't be the Olsan-Peru Import-Export Company by any chance?'

'How did you get hold of that information?'

'Just a guess. So I was right?'

'It's no secret.'

'No, I suppose not.'

'What have you found?' Walden asked. He sounded suspicious.

'Nothing much. Nothing definite anyway.'

'You're on to something, aren't you?'

'Oh, I wouldn't say that.'

'Have you found that girl?'

'What girl?'

'You know bloody well what girl. Melissa Lloyd of course. Who else?'

'Wouldn't I have told you if I had?'

'Damn you, Sam.' Walden was shouting into the telephone now. 'If you're holding out on us — '

'I'll be in touch,' Grant said, and rang off.

He thought about putting in a call to the office, but there was nothing he really wanted to tell Peking at this stage, so he decided to let it wait. He joined up again with Susan Sims and relieved her of the burden of the Inca.

'Now we'll go home,' he said.

* * *

There was no sound in the flat when they went in. There was no sign of the statuette that should have been there, either.

'Damn!' Grant said. 'She's flown.'

He blamed himself; he ought to have known she would take off as soon as he let her out of his sight. And yet he had done it; he had been fool enough to take the risk. Now he would have to start looking for her all over again. Hell.

He was still mentally cursing himself when Miss Sims said: 'Don't worry. She'th thtill here.'

She had gone straight to the bedroom door and opened it. Grant joined her and saw Melissa was in bed again and fast asleep. He remembered then that it was precisely what he himself had suggested she should do. The statuette was standing on the floor, so she must have carried it in there before turning in. Maybe she still thought it was valuable.

He gave a sigh of relief and stopped cursing himself. He had been right to trust her after all. 'Don't wake her,' he whispered. He tiptoed into the bedroom, picked up the statuette and tiptoed out again. Melissa stirred slightly but did not wake.

He put the statuette on the table in the sitting room and then he took the one he had bought out of its box and stood it beside the other. There was not a thing to choose between them; they were alike as a pair of front teeth with new crowns on them.

Susan Sims examined them first from one side and then the other. 'I don't thee the thlightetht differenth,' she said. 'Do you?'

'No,' Grant said. But there had to be a difference. Why otherwise would Olmedo have taken the trouble to cart one of them down to Westerton Old Hall and keep it under his bed? His firm was handling dozens, maybe hundreds, of the statuettes, so why pick one out for himself? It just did not make sense if the two on the table were indeed identical. So perhaps the one Olmedo had taken was the original, the rarity, the genuine antique from which all the others had been copied. But he doubted that; the thing looked no older; it was in mint condition; if it had been centuries old it would have had to have some blemishes on it somewhere.

He took it in his hands and examined it again, turning it this way and that; but there was nothing that he could see to distinguish it from the other, nothing at all. In fact, so alike were the two that it might be advisable to stow them away in their separate boxes and mark the containers before he could no longer remember which was which.

He said. 'I think you'd better wake Melissa. She'll probably like to know that her treasure is identical with the shop variety.'

Susan Sims went to the bedroom, and Miss Lloyd must have been a lot quicker at putting her clothes on than she had once been at taking them off, otherwise she would have beaten the music to the tape every time. She was dressed and in the sitting room in scarcely half a minute. She had not bothered about the wig and her hair was in a tangle, but she looked all right to Grant; she was the kind of girl who never needed to take a lot of pains to look good; she was just made that way.

She stared at the two statuettes on the table and walked right up to them and took a real hard look. Then she said in a voice that was hardly more than a whisper: 'Which is mine?'

'You mean the one you pinched?' Grant

said. 'It's on the right. The other cost twenty-five pounds at a shop in the Strand.'

'Like I told you it would,' Miss Sims put in.

'I can't believe it.'

'You've got to believe it,' Grant said. 'It's there in front of your eyes.'

'So it's true. He was fooling me.' She seemed suddenly dispirited, as though she had trusted in something and now found her trust had been betrayed. 'I would never have believed he would lie to me. Keep things from me, yes; that was to be expected. But not lie to me; not Enrique.'

'Well, it seems he did,' Grant said. 'And there's something else I think you ought to know.'

He thought she stiffened a little, perhaps preparing herself for some further disillusionment. 'Something else?'

'Olmedo was a partner in the firm that imports these things. They ship them from Peru by the cartload. So if he didn't know this one you took from the house down at Westerton was nothing out of the ordinary, who would?'

She gave a long sigh. 'I suppose you must be right. What are you going to do now?'

'Eventually you know I shall have to go to the police.'

'But not yet; not today. Please.'

He thought about it, and he could see no very immediate need to unburden himself to Sergeant Walden and Superintendent Kerrison. He could play around with it a bit longer and maybe something else would come to light. And besides, he still had to think about his duty to his client.

'All right,' he said, 'we'll leave it for another day or so. But I think it's time we had a word with Mr Sanchez.'

She stared at him as if she thought he had suddenly gone off the rails. 'Who on earth is Mr Sanchez?'

'You mean to say you don't know?'

She shook her head.

'Olmedo never mentioned him?'

'No.'

'I'm surprised. He really did keep his business out of his relationship with you, didn't he? Sanchez was his partner and he's taken charge of things now. He also happens to be the late Mr Olmedo's cousin and pretty narked about the way he was carved up.'

'Oh,' she said; and he guessed she was trying to work out how this might affect her. 'And why do you think we ought to go and have a word with him?'

'Because he's the man who's employing me to find you.'

She looked surprised, but also puzzled. 'Why should he want me found? I don't understand. What is it to him whether I'm found or not?'

'He wants to nail the men who killed his cousin and he's fed up with waiting for the police to do it. I think he would also like to take a bit of personal revenge.'

'Well, what can I do?'

'Just tell him what happened.'

'How will that help?'

'Possibly not at all. But it's what he wants. At least you'll be able to assure him you didn't have any part in the killing.'

Her eyes widened at this. 'You mean he thinks I had?'

'I believe he thinks you may have had. You can't blame him. He knows you were there on the night of the murder and that you disappeared afterwards. He's bound to think you could have been implicated.'

'Does anyone else believe that?' she asked.

He could tell she was thinking of the police, and maybe she was seeing enemies springing up on all sides. Certainly there was a hunted look in her eyes, and he felt sorry for her even though she had undoubtedly brought much of the trouble on herself.

'I don't know,' he said. 'It's possible. That's why it would be best to get it all cleared up as soon as we can. You do see that, don't you?'

'Yes,' she said, but still a little doubtfully, 'I suppose so.'

'And for a start you'll have a talk with Mr Sanchez?'

Again she answered with that hint of doubt, as though fearful of what she might be letting herself in for. 'I suppose so.'

'Good. Then I'll get in touch with him

and make the arrangements.'

'But you'll be there too,' she said quickly. 'I won't have to see him alone?'

'You want me to be there?'

'Yes. Oh, yes.'

He saw that she still felt the need of that shoulder to lean on, and since he had intended all along to hear what Sanchez would say to her, he was able to agree without hesitation.

'All right; I'll tag along.'

She seemed to relax a little. 'When will you fix it?'

'I'll get on the phone now and see if I can contact him.'

He tried the London number, and again he was lucky. Sanchez himself answered.

'I've found the lady,' Grant said.

'Ah!' He could detect the satisfaction in Sanchez's voice. A trace of excitement too, perhaps. 'Where is she now, Mr Grant?'

'At my flat. She's willing to talk to you.'

'And the police? You haven't informed them?'

'Not yet.'

'Good. No need to bring them in for the moment.'

'Where would you like Miss Lloyd to meet you?'

There was a brief pause while Sanchez appeared to be considering the question. Then he said: 'Why don't you bring her here? You have the address, don't you?'

'Yes.'

'So let me see. The time is now five minutes past four. How long will it take you to get here?'

'I've got one or two things to do first. Better give it an hour. You never know about the traffic.'

'Very well. I'll expect you soon after five o'clock.'

Grant went back to the sitting room and told the others what he had arranged.

'At his flat,' Melissa said. 'Where's that?'

Grant told her the address.

'Oh, my God!' she said. 'That's where Enrique used to live when he was in London.'

It was not altogether surprising. When Sanchez arrived from Peru it was only natural that he should take over Olmedo's quarters; it was the simplest thing to do. Why should he bother to hunt round for somewhere else to live when there was furnished accommodation waiting at his disposal?

'Does it bother you?' Grant asked. The place might have memories for her that she would prefer not to have revived. 'I could alter the arrangement if you'd rather not go there.'

'No,' she said, 'it doesn't matter. Let's keep it the way it is.'

'All right then. Now you'd better get yourself ready while I pack these things away.'

She turned and went into the bedroom, and Grant started putting the statuettes back in their boxes. He marked the boxes with a ball-point pen, inscribing on them the letters 'A' and 'B'. Box 'A' contained the statuette that had come from the Old Hall at Westerton, while the one from the shop in the Strand was in Box 'B'. He put box 'B' on the floor under the table.

Susan Sims was watching him. 'You thtill don't believe there ithn't any differenth between them, do you?'

'Let's put it this way,' he said. 'Let's just say I'm keeping an open mind for the present and I don't want to get them mixed up.'

'What are you going to do with model 'A'?'

He thought about it for a few moments. Then he said: 'I think it may as well go back to where it's been for the last few months. It should be safe enough there.'

'Thafe enough!' she said. 'Who do you think ith likely to thteal it?'

'Maybe nobody. But why take the chance?'

'Who would bother to run off with a whopping great bit of math-produthed pottery worth twenty-five poundth?'

'People steal things worth less than that.'

'Tho why hide only one of them?'

'Now you're being awkward.'

Yet he knew she could be right in saying that nobody would want to steal the statuette, since there had never been any proof that the men who had killed

Olmedo had been looking for it. It was just an idea that Melissa had got into her head and which she herself seemed to have abandoned now. But he took it nevertheless. He put it in the Cortina and carted it round to the lock-up garage and stowed it in the boot of the MGB.

She was ready when he got back to the flat. She was wearing the blonde wig again and had got herself into a brown denim skirt with a jacket to match. She looked worth anybody's money, and the thought crossed his mind that when Sanchez saw her he might have the bright idea of taking over something else from his late lamented cousin.

'Okay,' he said, 'we may as well be on our way.'

'Are you taking me too?' Susan Sims asked.

'Mr Sanchez didn't invite you.'

'Did you tell him about me?'

'No.'

'Then it'th hardly thurprithing, ith it? He doethn't even know I exitht.'

'Do you want to go?'

'No, thank you.'

‘Then why make such a fuss about it?’
‘Who’th making a futh about it?’
Grant decided not to answer that. He conducted Miss Lloyd out of the flat and left Miss Sims to her own resources.

10

Hard Men

It was in the Mayfair district and it was luxurious enough to make Grant's flat look like something that had been taken over by squatters. Sanchez had a servant; a lean, coppery-faced character with a nose like an eagle's beak and coarse black hair, who opened the door to them and looked as though he might have been brought over from Peru. Sanchez addressed him as Diego, but Grant would have said that some of his ancestors might well have had Indian names. He wondered whether the man had been there in Olmedo's time, but no hint of any mutual recognition passed between him and Melissa, so it seemed probable that he had been installed by Sanchez.

Introduced to Melissa, Sanchez said he was charmed to meet her; which could have been true. His eyes were certainly giving her a thorough going-over.

'I have been wishing to have a little talk with you for some time.'

'So Mr Grant said.'

'Yes, of course. Now do please sit down.' He indicated chairs with a flutter of plump fingers. They were the sort that anyone could buy — anyone who had the spare two hundred pounds to spend on an armchair. There was a Bang and Olufsen television set strategically placed, while a fairly comprehensive array of wines and spirits made a tasteful display on a side-table. There were two or three paintings by artists who had not quite made it yet but were obviously on the way to the big money league, and the carpet was the genuine article all the way from the mysterious Orient.

They sat down. Mr Sanchez offered refreshment. Grant declined; it was not a social call; they were there on business. Melissa, possibly taking her cue from him, refused also. Grant thought she seemed uneasy; her gaze kept wandering round the room, almost as though she were looking for someone else; someone who ought to have been there but was not, and never would be again.

'Well, then,' Sanchez said, 'if you will take nothing, perhaps we had better get down to the purpose of this interview. You, Miss Lloyd, were, I believe, present on the night when my cousin was murdered.'

She nodded, but said nothing.

'Would you like to tell me about it?'

'I've told Mr Grant.'

'But now I should like to hear it.' Sanchez's voice was soft and persuasive, almost purring. It struck Grant that he was rather cat-like in more ways than one; he had cat-like movements and his eyes were sleepy but watchful. Like a cat he might wait patiently for the right moment to come along and then pounce with deadly effect.

Melissa shot a glance at Grant, a kind of appeal.

'The revised version,' Grant said.

'All of it?'

'All of it.'

She took a breath and began. It was basically the same as she had told it to him the second time, with no essential changes; which would seem to indicate that that was the way it had in fact happened. Sanchez listened without making any interruption, though Grant thought his eyes narrowed slightly when she came to the bit about the statuette which Olmedo had kept hidden under the bed. But he heard her out to the end and then sat rubbing his chin reflectively.

After a while he said: 'Did you get a good view of the men?'

'Reasonably good.'

'You think you would know them again if you saw them?'

'I am sure of it.'

'And that is why you ran away and went into hiding? Because you were afraid those men would be looking for you and would want to kill you?'

'Yes.'

Sanchez nodded. 'It is possible. So now you must do all you can to help us find them.'

'What can I do? I've told you all I know.'

'Suppose you describe the men. You can do that?'

Grant knew from experience that eye-witnesses were seldom good at descriptions, and Melissa Lloyd was no better than the next person. She remembered the black leather coat and the trench-coat; she remembered that the man in the leather coat had dark hair, thinning on top, and a wide, bony face; she remembered that the man in the trench-coat had thick hair which had turned grey but not because of age.

'I don't think he was more than thirty; he didn't look old except for the hair and he walked like a young man.'

That was about as far as she was able to go in the descriptive line, but even at that it might have been enough to put Walden and Kerrison on the right track, especially if she had gone down to the Yard and had taken a look at some of the mug-shots. So maybe it was time to stop playing around, time to give Walden the tip. It would be the best thing for her; it would put her right with the law. And if Sanchez didn't like it, that was just too bad. As far as Sanchez was concerned he had kept his side of the bargain; he had brought the girl to him first.

Sanchez went off abruptly on to a fresh tack. 'That statuette you took up to the roof — you thought it was very valuable?'

'I certainly thought so then,' Melissa said. 'Enrique told me it was. Of course I know now he was just kidding. It must have been some big practical joke, I suppose.'

'So you don't believe it now?'

'That it's valuable? Of course not. You can buy an exactly identical one for twenty-five pounds at a shop in the Strand. Probably other shops too.'

Sanchez smiled. 'I expect you can.'

He should know, Grant thought; it's his firm that brings them into the country. But he said nothing; there was no point in telling Sanchez that he knew about the Olsan-Peru Import-Export Company.

Sanchez appeared to lose interest in the questioning. Possibly he was disappointed; possibly he had hoped to get more from the girl and felt that it had all been rather a waste of time.

He said: 'Well, if you really won't take any refreshment I don't think I need keep you any longer. It was good of you to come.' He stood up and rang a bell and the dark-skinned servant with the beaked nose was there in an instant. 'Diego will show you out.'

They were about to go when he thought of something else. 'Oh, Miss Lloyd, if I should wish to get in touch with you again, where can I contact you?'

She looked at Grant, hesitating.

Grant said: 'Miss Lloyd is staying at my place for the present.'

'Ah, then perhaps you will be so kind as to let me have the address.'

Grant was not sure he wished to let Sanchez have his address, but he could think of no plausible excuse for not doing so, and he gave it. Sanchez made a note of it.

'I take it, Mr Grant, that you are still working for me?'

'You want me to do that?'

'Surely, Mr Grant, surely.'

Grant thought of telling him again that it was a job for the police and that it was not his line, but he thought also of Mr Peking's disapproval if he choked off a client as wealthy as this one and he decided to give it a bit more of a run. After all, there was no need for him to come into physical contact with the men, was there? Sanchez had only said locate them. And the odds were still pretty heavily against his locating them anyway.

'I'll do what I can,' he said.

Sanchez laid a plump pink hand on his arm, which he found a trifle distasteful. 'Of course you will. And I am sure it will be all that I could ask for.'

After that they got out of the flat with the help of the dark manservant and went down in the lift and found the Cortina where they had left it. Grant unlocked it and they got in.

'Do you want to go anywhere in particular?' he asked.

She shook her head. He thought she was not looking very happy. He was not terribly happy himself. He could see nothing much to be happy about.

'Then we may as well go back to the flat.'

* * *

Susan Sims was out when they got there. She had left no note to say where she had gone or when she was likely to be back, so he took it that he could expect her when he saw her. Maybe she had gone to see a film.

He thought about ringing Scotland Yard and asking for Detective Sergeant Walden or even Detective Superintendent Kerrison, because maybe the sooner he put them in the picture the better for his future standing with that particular department and the more likely he was to get some co-operation when he needed it. But he looked at his watch and it was past seven, and if they had not already knocked off they might not be any too pleased to get some fresh work coming in at that hour, so maybe it would be better to leave it until the morning after all.

He was aware of a grumbling in his stomach and he remembered that neither of them had eaten since lunch.

'I don't know about you,' he said, 'but I'm hungry. Would you like me to see what there is in the way of grub?'

She was still looking pretty miserable but she raised no objection, so he went into the kitchen and opened a tin of Spam and found some tomatoes in the refrigerator and a bottle of red wine that had miraculously not been opened. She came in while he was doing it and offered to lend a hand, which was something he never believed in refusing, and pretty soon there was a not at all bad makeshift meal lined up.

They ate at the kitchen bench, sitting on a couple of stools side by side, and gradually she became rather more cheerful and he felt a little happier himself. It was the first time they had had that kind of tête-à-tête, and it might have been the wine loosening her tongue or simply a need to confide in someone who would lend a sympathetic ear, but before long she was talking about herself and giving him a fresh insight into what made her tick. It had always been her ambition to go on the stage, to become a great actress; but of course she had never had the chance to go to drama school. She had got into provincial rep for a time, but it had led nowhere, and so eventually the great acting dream had ended up with strip-tease in sweaty little joints like the Peel of Belles and the Deuce of Diamonds. She drank some more wine and went back further and told him about the man who had seduced her when she was thirteen, of the work she had done for the pornographic photographer, and then of life at the commune.

'You liked it there?'

'It was the only time I really felt clean,' she said. 'Clean right through.' And he knew she was not referring to the pump over the sink.

She began to cry a little. He put his arm round her and suddenly she was clinging to him, pressed hard against him and shaking. And he was thinking: This won't do, Sammy, this won't do at all. It was all very well to lend her a shoulder to lean on, but this seemed to be leaning a shade too heavily. Nevertheless, he found himself kissing her and not finding it so terribly unpleasant either; rather enjoyable in fact.

And 'Sam,' she kept saying. 'Oh, Sam, hold me, hold me.'

So he held her, and it might have gone further than that if he had not heard the door of the flat open and someone walk in. He guessed it must be Susan Sims back home, and he got himself disentangled from Miss Lloyd in double-quick time and walked out of the kitchen trying to look innocent. But there was no need to bother about his looks because it was not Miss Sims; it was a couple of male visitors he had never seen before, and he supposed he must have left the door unlocked and they had just walked in without so much as a knock. Either that or they knew how to work the lock with a strip of celluloid or a piece of stout wire; and when he had taken a good look at them he thought it more than likely that they did.

One of them had a gun in his right hand. The other one appeared to be left-handed; at least that was the hand he used to haul the flick-knife out of his pocket. The blade sprang out with a snap and he held it waist-high, tilted slightly upward. He had dark hair, thinning at the forehead and crown, a shapeless kind of face and a slack, moist mouth; his nose was broad and slightly flattened. The other man had grey hair, but his face was young-looking. He was a smiler; the smile hung loose about his mouth but never rose as far as his eyes. The eyes had a washed-out appearance, as though the colour had gone out of them at the same time as it had faded from his hair. His skin was as pale as lard.

The dark-haired man weaved little patterns in the air with the tip of the knife. Grant could imagine it tracing the same kind of patterns on Olmedo's body. It was not a pleasant thought, because a man who would do that sort of thing once would probably be quite prepared to do it again.

He heard Melissa come out of the kitchen and give a squawk when she saw the men.

'Oh, God!' she said. 'It's them.'

The one with the gun in his hand just looked at her and went on smiling.

The one with the knife said: 'That's right, sweetheart. It's us.' The blade traced more patterns in the air; delicate patterns, fine as old lace.

'What do you want?' Grant said. But he knew.

It was the one with the young face and the grey hair who answered. 'Suppose you guess, Mr Grant; suppose you guess.'

'So you know my name.'

'Oh, we know your name. We know hers and all. Melissa Lloyd as ever was. That right, gorgeous?'

She just stared at him. She seemed scared. And she had reason to be. She knew them, and that was dangerous knowledge.

'Maybe I'll tell you our names,' the smiling man said. 'Just to make it all nice and matey. I'm Brad and he's — well, you can call him Slicer.'

Grant looked at the one they could call Slicer. The knife was still moving, never still, the blade silver-bright and razor sharp. No need to ask why they could call him that.

'I didn't hear you make that guess,'

Brad said. 'Maybe I'm going deaf or something.'

'I didn't make a guess,' Grant said. He looked at the gun in the man's hand. It was a Walther PPK automatic.

'It's loaded,' the man said.

Grant smiled faintly. 'I don't doubt it. But I'm still not guessing.'

'Let's not play games,' Slicer said. 'The sod knows what we've come for. What she took from Olmedo's 'ouse down in the sticks.' He pointed the knife at Melissa with a kind of stabbing motion and she shrank away.

'What did she take?'

'A bit of pottery, that's what; a little statue like. As if you didn't know.'

'And what makes you think it's here?'

'She's 'ere, ain' she? Where else would it be?'

'What's your interest in the statuette?'

'Never mind what our interest is. We want it, see?'

'Oh, I see that,' Grant said. 'The question is, will you get it?'

'We'll get it all right.' The knife traced more airy patterns. 'And I'd say the question is this, do we get it the easy way or the ’ard way? And I don’t ’ave to tell you what the ’ard way is. You can figure that out for yourself if you ain’t weak in the ’ead.’

‘The hard way for you, friend,’ Brad put in, smiling. ‘Not for us. Easy for us, easy.’

‘Tell them,’ Melissa said urgently. ‘Tell them, Sam. You know they can make you.’

Grant agreed. ‘I think you’re right.’ He walked to the table and hauled out the cardboard box. ‘Here it is.’

Slicer put his knife away, opened the box and pulled out the statuette.

‘Is that what you were looking for?’ Grant asked.

‘That’s the boy,’ Slicer said. He appeared surprised that it should have been so easy. He even sounded a shade suspicious, as though he felt there must be some catch. ‘You didn’t ’ide it very well. Anybody could’ve found it.’

‘I wasn’t expecting anyone to try. It’s not valuable, you know.’

‘No? So why did she take it?’

Melissa was silent, and Grant wondered whether she realised that this was the statuette that had come from the shop. She had been in the bedroom when he had taken the other one away and stowed it in the MGB and he had not bothered to tell her.

'She made a mistake,' he said.

Slicer gave a jeering laugh. 'So now we're going to make the same mistake.' He put the statuette back in its box. 'Only we don't think it is a mistake. Not really. Nor you don't neither, do you, Mr Grant? Or do we call you Sam?'

'You can call me what you like as long as it's decent. Are you going now?'

'We're going.'

'And you're coming with us,' Brad said. 'You and the lady.'

Grant was not surprised. There were two people in the room who could have put the police on to them and they were not likely to leave matters like that. He regretted now that he had not put through that call to Scotland Yard; it looked as though his procrastination might prove very costly — both to him and the girl. And he knew there was no way out of the situation; these were hard men — what they had done to Olmedo was proof of that — and one of them had a gun and the other had a knife. It would be foolish to imagine they were not fully prepared to use the weapons if it became necessary.

'Okay,' he said. 'If you say so.'

Slicer grinned. 'There's a man as knows what's good for 'im. Sensible, that's what you are, Sam boy; real sensible.'

Grant was not so sure about that, but he let it go.

11

Wrong Box

They made him carry the statuette down the stairs and out to the car. Maybe they figured that with his hands full he was less likely to try any tricks. They went down with the girl leading the way and Slicer just behind her. He stayed very close to her and he had the flick-knife in his hand with the blade retracted; but he could have used it in a moment if she had made a false move. But she showed no inclination to do anything of the kind; she knew about the knife and wanted no trouble. She probably realised as well as Grant did that they were heading for trouble anyway, but she was not eager to bring it any nearer.

Grant was about two steps behind Slicer with Brad close behind him. Brad had his right hand inside his jacket as though he were feeling for his wallet or maybe scratching his chest, but it was the gun he had in there and he could have pulled it out very quickly if he had wanted to. Grant thought about throwing the statuette at Slicer's head and knocking him down the stairs. It would have knocked Melissa down as well and would have caused a lot of confusion during which he might have tackled Brad without getting himself shot in the process. But it was too risky. He might have tried it if there had been any other people about, but there was no one. There never was anyone when you really wanted someone; that was life.

So he was still carrying the box containing the Inca statuette when they reached the street. The Cortina was parked by the kerb, but he guessed they would not be travelling in that; which at least would mean a bit of saving on the petrol, though that might turn out to be of only academic interest. Walden had told him that bread and cheese was no use to a dead man, and the same could apply to saving petrol. And that really was a nice gloomy thought to come into the head.

It was raining lightly and there was a man hurrying past on the other side of the road with an umbrella held above his head. He was about as much use to Grant as a sore thumb. The other car was parked just ahead of the Cortina; it was a big grey Citröen. Slicer opened the front door and told Melissa to get in. She did so and he shut the door and ran round the front of the car and got into the driving seat. Brad opened the rear door with his left hand; apparently they had not bothered to lock the doors.

'Get in,' he said.

Grant got in and put the box on the floor. Brad followed him and Slicer had the Citröen moving before he had completed shutting the door.

'Where are we going?' Grant asked.

'For a little trip,' Brad said. 'Into the country.'

'Isn't it a bit late in the day for that?'

'It depends what you're going into the country for.' Still with that smile; always that damned smile hovering round his mouth. 'There's some kinds of business you can't beat the country for.'

Slicer gave a low chuckle. 'Like farming.'

Grant doubted whether Slicer's knowledge of farming, even if added to that of Brad, would have filled the correspondence space on a picture postcard if written in large block capitals. They were strictly the city type, brought up with the concrete and the pin-tables, the neon lights and the betting shops.

'They tell me you're a country boy yourself,' Brad remarked.

Grant wondered who had told him that. Somebody must have been interested enough to pry into his background.

'That's so.'

'Maybe you should have stayed there. I hear it's a healthy way of life.'

'It can be.'

'Whereas your present way of life is a different bag of tricks altogether. That can be very unhealthy indeed.'

'I've managed to stay pretty fit so far.'

Slicer chuckled again. 'Ah, but for 'ow much longer? That's what you better ask yourself, Sam boy; 'ow much longer will it last?'

Brad smiled at him. 'He's right, you know. You could be coming to a very sickly period in your life.' He pressed the muzzle of the gun into Grant's side. 'It's even doubtful if you'll survive it.' The smile stayed there on his mouth but the eyes were like a snake's. Grant wondered whether it was possible that he was a psychopath. Slicer, too, if it came to that. Car ride to the country with a brace of psychos. Sweet thought.

Melissa was sitting very still and quiet. She was probably scared out of her wits. She knew what the score was; she had worked it out long ago. This was her worst dream come true; this was the nightmare turned to fact. Grant felt sorry for her. He felt sorry for himself too. There was a lot to feel sorry about.

When they were clear of Greater London Slicer let the Citröen go. It was a road Grant knew; he seemed to have been using it fairly frequently the last few days. But still he was a bit slow in picking up the message. Indeed, it was not until they reached Bury St Edmunds that it really got through to him. When he discovered which road they were taking on the other side of Bury he felt pretty sure what their destination was going to be. And then he had to start changing his ideas about a whole stack of things and he began to curse himself for having been so blind, so damned gullible.

It had grown dark by this time. Nobody was talking and he wondered whether it was possible that Brad could have fallen asleep. If he could get the gun everything would be all right; he would have the whip-hand, and by God he would use it.

He turned his head cautiously. Brad certainly looked as if he might be asleep; he was leaning back on the seat and his chin appeared to be resting on his chest. It was impossible in the dim light inside the Citröen to tell for certain whether his eyes were closed or not, but Grant believed they were. So perhaps the soporific motion of the car had made him doze off. Slicer was concentrating on his driving and taking no notice of anything that might be going on behind him. It was an opportunity not to be missed, since it might never come again.

Grant turned from the waist, bringing himself square on to Brad. Still the grey-haired man did not move. Grant tried to figure out where exactly the gun was. In the pocket of Brad's jacket perhaps. He stretched out his right hand, feeling for the pocket.

Brad's hand came out with the gun in it. The muzzle dug viciously into Grant's ribs, freezing his movement, halting him in the act.

'Don't try it. Don't even think about it, Sam. It could kill you.'

Slicer's voice came floating back, though he had not turned his head. 'What's 'e doing?'

'Being clever,' Brad said. 'But not clever enough. He thought he could catch me napping.'

Slicer laughed. 'That'll be the day.'

The pistol shifted away from Grant's ribs and he was not sorry about that. Such a weapon could be fired by accident, and at that range there was no chance of the bullet missing its mark.

'I thought you wanted waking.'

'I'll bet you did,' Brad said.

The Citröen pressed on smoothly, making light of the distance. They came to the turning to the left and Slicer took the car on to the minor road, and Grant knew his guess had been correct. Not long after that they came to the outlying farmhouse and the cottages, the church with the square tower and the graveyard full of dark shadows which might have been the ghosts of people buried there long ago, the inn with a lamp over the door, the garage, closed for the night, the shop and the duck-pond.

'Been here before?' Brad asked.

'Yes,' Grant said.

'And Miss Lloyd too, I shouldn't wonder.'

She said nothing, but there was an impression of tenseness about her, as though she were keyed up, preparing herself for some ordeal.

Slicer turned the car off into the lane, and the beech trees flitted past like twin columns of tall guardsmen. And then they were on the gravel in front of the Old

Hall and he could not even have a doubt any more.

It was not Mrs Jenner who let them in; she was no doubt in her own home. It was the dark-haired, dark-skinned man-servant named Diego. It was almost like sleight of hand; only a few hours earlier he had let them into the flat in Mayfair; now here he was, utterly impassive, carrying out the same duty at the Old Hall, Westerton. But the explanation was simple and there was no magic about it; Sanchez had come down ahead of them and had brought his servant with him.

He was in the drawing room and he greeted them with the suave politeness of a man receiving guests who had perhaps been invited for the weekend. He did not go quite so far as to say it was good of them to come, but he seemed to imply as much.

'So they were your gorillas all the time,' Grant said. 'It wasn't them you were paying me to find. You could have laid your hands on them any time you wanted, because they were working for you.'

'Well, yes,' Sanchez admitted with a deprecatory smile, 'I must confess I did rather mislead you. It was Miss Lloyd I really wished you to find; the other part was just a bluff. And you did find her; you carried out that assignment most expeditiously; I have nothing but praise for your professional skill.'

'Never mind the praise. Let's hear about Mr Olmedo. What happened to all that cousinly love there was between you?'

'Ah, that.' Sanchez made a little gesture with the smooth, soft palms of his hands, a gesture of rejection. 'Such things cannot survive a double-cross.'

'He double-crossed you?'

'He cheated me. It is the same thing.'

'In what way?'

'That is none of your business,' Sanchez said. And then: 'But there; why should I not tell you? You will never have the chance to repeat it. He contended — quite falsely — that I owed him a certain sum of money, and to get even he took for himself something that was strictly speaking a mutual possession; I had as large an interest in it as he did. His intention was to cheat me out of my share of the profit on this item and keep it all for himself, in order, as he put it, to make matters square between us. He thought I would lie down under this kind of treatment and carry on with our partnership as if nothing had happened, but I am not that sort of man, Mr Grant. I came over to this country to reason with him; I gave him every chance to reconsider, but it was useless; he refused to see reason. I was therefore compelled to take the necessary steps to safeguard my own interests.'

'Rather drastic steps, wouldn't you say?'

'But justified.'

'For the sake of your share in the profit from one Inca statuette when you were dealing in hundreds, maybe even thousands?'

'There is a principle in these affairs that has to be maintained.'

'So you acted on principle?'

'You might say that. I was of course

back in Peru when the murder took place.'

Grant wondered whether Sanchez could really be telling the truth. It seemed preposterous; yet why make up such a story? So, accepting it as true, Olmedo had died because of an argument between cousins, a disagreement about money. It was not unprecedented. Yet that it should have occurred by reason of such a trivial amount was scarcely credible. There had to be more to it than Sanchez had revealed.

Diego had been sent out to fetch the cardboard box from the car. He brought it in and set it on the floor. Sanchez looked at it and then at Brad.

'Where had he hidden it?'

'Under the table,' Brad said.

Sanchez roared with laughter; it seemed a great joke to him. 'The table! Then it was not really hidden at all.'

'I wasn't expecting anyone to steal it,' Grant said. 'For something worth so little, why bother.'

Sanchez laughed again. 'So little! Of course not.' He walked over to the box, lifted out the statuette and stood it on a side-table. 'What is it but a piece of baked clay?' He passed his hands over it in a kind of caress. 'Yet more than that. So much, much more.'

Melissa Lloyd was watching him in terrified fascination. Possibly she was trying to see in him some hint of that kinship with the man who had loved her, with whom she had shared this house as well as the flat in London. And maybe she could see nothing; nothing that would give her reason for the slightest hope. Sanchez might be polite, smooth, even urbane, but he was none the less cruel and ruthless for that. He might not have carved up his cousin Enrique with his own plump hands, but he had employed the men who had done it and he was as guilty as they were.

Suddenly his fingers ceased their caressing movements and he seemed to stiffen. He turned the statuette on its side and examined the base. Then he wheeled round and all the urbanity had vanished.

'So,' he said in a low, savage voice, 'there has been another double-cross.

Which of you did it? Or are you all in it together? Is it a conspiracy?'

Brad and Slicer looked bewildered. Melissa glanced at Grant as though she had a suspicion of what had happened but could not be certain.

'Double-cross?' Brad said. 'How do you mean?'

'I mean this is not the right statuette.'

'It was the only one as was there,' Slicer said.

Sanchez turned on Grant. 'So it was you who did the switch. You and the lady perhaps.' He seemed to remember something. 'Of course. That shop in the Strand you spoke about. You bought one there — this one.' He stabbed a finger at the statuette on the table as though he had begun to hate it. 'And then you hid the other one and stood this under the table.' His eye was caught by the box and he pounced on it. 'And you marked the box. Here is the letter 'B'. So where is box 'A', Mr Grant? Where is it?' He was glaring; a vein was throbbing in his forehead; his face was suffused with passion. 'Tell me.'

'Now wait a minute,' Grant said. 'Why

get so heated? Suppose we do a deal. You keep this one and I keep the other. They're identical, you know.'

'Don't be a fool.' Sanchez was almost shouting now, spraying saliva, stamping his foot. 'You know they are not identical; that is why you switched them. What other reason could you have had?'

'Well, I must admit I thought there had to be a difference — unless Mr Olmedo was a very big practical joker. But I didn't know for certain, not until now. So now you tell me, what's so special about the other one?'

'Never mind what's so special about it. Where is it?'

'In a safe place. Don't worry.'

'It is you who should worry,' Sanchez said; but he was calming down. 'You should remember what happened to my dear cousin Enrique when he was obstinate.'

Grant heard Melissa utter a stifled cry and heard the metallic click of the knife. He turned his head and saw that Slicer was holding it in his hand, tracing those invisible patterns in the air.

'You will be sensible of course,' Sanchez said. 'You will not be obstinate.'

Grant looked into Sanchez's eyes and saw how cold they were. 'If you put it like that.'

'Now please tell us where the statuette is.'

'Back in London.'

'Naturally. But London is a big city. You must be rather more specific.'

'If you want it I shall have to fetch it myself.'

Sanchez gave a smile. 'Oh, no, Mr Grant, that will not do; it will not do at all. Do you think we can let you go running away to fetch it? I ask you, would we ever see you back here again?'

'You can send someone with me.'

'I think it would be better if you told us where it is and someone else went and fetched it.'

'I could tell where it is and they would still not be able to find it; not in a month.'

'How is that?'

'You have to know the place. A description would be no good at all. I tell you, I'm the only one who can find it, because I'm the one who hid it.'

'I think maybe you are bluffing, amigo.'

'You can think what you damned well please, amigo.'

Sanchez was silent for a few moments, gazing speculatively at Grant. Then he said: 'Very well; you will go and fetch it and Brad will go with you. Diego also. You' — he pointed at Slicer — 'will stay here and look after Miss Lloyd.'

Slicer glanced at the knife in his hand and grinned suddenly, as though in the expectation of some enjoyable experience. Melissa again shrank away from him and Grant felt a shade uneasy. Suppose Slicer jumped the gun.

'You'd better make sure he doesn't touch her. If she comes to any harm — '

'What will you do?' Sanchez asked with a sneer. 'Please don't make any threats you are in no position to carry out. Anyway, you may rest assured we shall take good care of Miss Lloyd, very good care indeed.'

There was more of menace than assurance in his words, Grant thought. He looked at Melissa and saw her wide, terrified eyes fixed on him as if imploring him not to leave her there; and he hated doing it, but there was no other way.

'It'll be all right,' he said. 'Don't worry.'

He might as well have told her to stop growing older; there would have been about as much chance of her following the advice; nobody ever yet stopped worrying on demand. And he knew she had good cause to worry; the way Slicer handled that knife gave no encouragement; it was obvious that he enjoyed using it, loved it. True, Sanchez would be there, but could Sanchez be depended on to restrain his man? Could he control Slicer if it came to the pinch? And even if he could, would he want to? After all, he was as deeply involved in Olmedo's murder as the other two and had as much interest in removing possible witnesses for the prosecution. But maybe he would not be in too great a hurry; maybe he would wait until he had his hands on the other statuette. Grant could only hope so.

'Now,' Sanchez said, 'you had better be on your way. You have quite a long journey to make. Really you would have saved yourself and us a lot of trouble if you had not played this foolish little trick of switching the boxes. You must have known you would never get away with it.'

'I thought it might provide you with some innocent entertainment. Not that you would know much about innocence, I suppose.'

Sanchez frowned slightly. 'You are being clever again. It doesn't help you.'

'It wasn't intended to.'

'And if you're thinking you may give these two men the slip, forget it.' He looked at Brad. 'You have the gun?'

Brad hauled the pistol out of his pocket and showed it to Sanchez, the smile hovering round his mouth. 'He won't get away.'

'And there is Diego also.'

'What does he use?' Grant asked. 'A gun or a knife?'

'Neither. But don't let that tempt you to try conclusions. He could break your arm.'

Grant looked at the silent manservant with the beaked nose and coppery skin. 'Maybe I could break his.'

The man's face was expressionless; his deep-set eyes regarded Grant without rancour. He was probably the kind who would obey orders and that was all; if he had to break somebody's arm he would do it because it was necessary, but there would be no personal feelings involved. A cold fish no doubt, but probably as deadly as either Brad or Slicer in his own passionless way.

'Let's go,' Brad said. He made a gesture with the pistol. 'Time's money.'

Grant doubted whether there would be any money in it for him; but he obeyed the order; a man with a gun had a lot of authority. He had a last glimpse of Melissa as he went out of the room, and he thought he had never seen anyone look so utterly tragic. He felt like a rat, walking out on her; but what else could he do?

Slicer was still tracing patterns with the knife.

12

A Bit of Digging

They took the Citröen. This time Brad did the driving. Grant sat in the back with Diego. The manservant might have had qualities of which Grant was not aware, but a gift for conversation was certainly not one of them, or if it was, he was not putting it on view just then. He sat there, silent and scarcely moving in his sober dark suit, like someone lost in contemplation.

Not that Grant had any desire to exchange small talk with Diego; it was very doubtful indeed whether they had any interests in common. What were the interests of a Peruvian manservant? He was damned if he knew. He had other things on his mind anyway.

The rain had stopped and the moon was up. They got on to the main road after a while and Brad was soon pushing the big Citröen even harder than Slicer had done. Maybe he was keen to get the job finished so that he could go to bed and catch some sleep; but he was not likely to get much in that line before morning. Grant himself had had no sleep the previous night and only a couple of hours or so on a sofa since then. In the circumstances, therefore, and with no disturbance likely to come from his silent companion on the left, he decided that he might as well take a little rest while he had the chance. He leaned back in the corner of the seat, closed his eyes, and was asleep almost at once.

He woke a few times, but nothing had changed; the Citröen was still pushing along at a good pace and Diego was still silent and motionless in his own corner, sitting there like someone watching at the bedside of a sick friend. Only there was no friendship in this relationship. There might be some sickness coming up, but that was quite another matter.

Later he must have drifted off into a pretty deep sleep, and the next thing he knew was that he was being shaken roughly and that somebody was telling him to wake up. He opened his eyes and discovered that the car had stopped. Brad had turned his head and was looking back at him, and he was the one who had been telling him to wake up. It was Diego who had been doing the shaking.

'Where are we?' he asked.

'Home,' Brad said. 'Your home, pal.'

He was not lying, either. Grant, now that he had become fully awake, could see the parked Cortina a few yards ahead and the house on the right. There was a light showing in one of the second-floor windows which he knew belonged to his own flat, so he guessed that Susan Sims had come home and was maybe sitting up and wondering where in hell he and Melissa had got to. Maybe thinking all kinds of wrong things and getting pretty mad at him for not leaving a message to say where he had gone. He looked at his watch and saw that it was around half-past one. She would surely be mad.

'Well?' Brad said, and he sounded impatient. 'Do we just sit here or do we get out and fetch what we came for?'

'It's not here,' Grant said.

That wiped the smile off Brad's face, which was some kind of achievement, he supposed. It proved that the thing was not a fixture.

'What d'you mean, not here?'

'I mean it's not here. That's plain English, isn't it?'

'So where in hell is it?'

'Somewhere else.'

'You don't say.' Brad was putting in the sarcasm. 'So now do you think it would be asking too much for you to tell me where we go from here?'

'Not too much at all. We go to my garage.'

'Where's that?'

'I'll direct you. Turn right at the end of this road, then first left. It's not far.'

Brad started the car and in a very short while they were in the cul-de-sac where the lock-up garages were. Grant still had the key with him, and when he got out of the Citröen he took a look one way and the other and there was not a soul about; just a gloomy little stretch of road that had not dried out after the rain and a street-lamp or two and one parked car — the Citröen. It was as depressing as a fun fair on a wet Sunday afternoon.

Brad had the pistol in his fist and Diego had got out of the car as well. They were taking no chances.

'What was all that blarney you gave us about the place being hard to find?' Brad said. 'You could have given me the key and I could have come straight here. Why didn't you say the thing was in your garage?'

'Because it isn't.'

'Then why are we here?'

'To get the spade.'

'What spade?'

'The spade I used when I buried it.'

'Oh, so it's buried?'

'If it wasn't I wouldn't need a spade, would I?'

'You've caused us a lot of trouble, one way and another. This had better be on the level.'

'Oh, it's on the level,' Grant said. He turned the key in the lock and opened the garage door and went in and switched the light on.

Brad stared at the red MGB. 'So this is where you stowed the lady's car. You're a cunning bastard, you are.'

'It had to be stowed somewhere. Doesn't do these open sports models any good to stand out in all weathers. Didn't you know that?'

'To say nothing of the coppers taking an interest in it.'

'There was that too,' Grant admitted. He walked to the far end of the garage where there was a spade hanging on a nail in the wall. He took the spade down, and Brad was watching him and keeping his distance, the idea having probably come into his mind that a spade could be a very lethal weapon. Diego had not come into the garage; he was standing in the doorway.

There was a workbench on one side. Grant laid the spade on the bench and pulled open a drawer.

'Now what are you up to?' Brad demanded in a suspicious tone of voice.

'I'm looking for some insulation tape.'

'What do you want that for?'

'The spade handle is splintering a bit; I

got a splinter in my hand last time I used it. I thought I'd bind it with the tape.'

'Well, hurry,' Brad said. 'We don't have all night.'

Grant found the roll of tape and bound part of the spade handle. He cut the tape with an old knife that was lying on the bench and slipped the roll into his pocket. He picked up the spade.

'Okay, I'm ready now.'

'And about time, too.'

He closed and locked the garage and they all got back into the Citröen.

'Where now?' Brad asked.

Grant told him. Brad got the car moving again. Diego had said nothing.

It was about half a mile away, a piece of waste ground that had once been the garden of a house. The house was decaying and had had squatters in it, but it had become too bad even for them. They had to get in through a gap in a fence, and the moonlight revealed some ragged shrubs and a litter of tin cans and other junk. Grant stopped and looked about him as though getting his bearings.

'You sure made it difficult,' Brad said.

'When I hide something I like to be sure it stays hidden until I come for it.'

He walked over to a sheet of rusty corrugated-iron and dragged it to one side. The ground underneath was hard and stony, but he began to dig. Brad stood with the pistol in his hand about five paces away, watching. Diego was a pace or two to Brad's left.

'You're sure that's the place?' Brad said.

Grant leaned on the spade. 'I'm sure.'

'How deep did you go?'

'A foot or two.'

He began to dig again. The ground really was hard; he could have used a pick. Brad edged a little closer.

'That ground doesn't look like it's been dug recently. How do you know it's the right place?'

'The corrugated-iron was there to mark it.'

'Maybe somebody shifted it.'

'No; this is where I buried the thing.'

He went on with his digging, making slow progress. He could sense that Brad was becoming more and more impatient.

The man came closer still; he was standing almost on the edge of the hole, staring down into it.

'That's not been dug up for years. You won't find anything there.'

'Think not?' Grant said. 'Well, maybe you're right at that.'

He swung the spade suddenly in a narrow arc and the flat of the blade struck Brad on the head. It was done so quickly that the man had not even begun to move. The pistol fell from his hand and he went down without a sound.

Grant thought of reaching for the gun and thought again, because Diego was a quick thinker and was coming at him fast. Diego came in with a flying kick that was aimed at his pelvis and would have done a lot of damage if it had gone home; but he turned in time and the toe-cap of Diego's shoe caught him just below the left hip. It felt like a hammer hitting him, and he staggered and there was a burning pain in his hip and all the way down his thigh. But there was no time to think about that, no time to think about anything but Diego coming at him again, as bouncy as an Olympic gymnast, and maybe trying for the pelvis again, and maybe even getting on the mark this time if he didn't do something about it — and quick.

He shifted his stance and swung backhanded with the spade, and it got home; it caught Diego just above the waist. He gave a grunt and it stopped him for a moment. But he was one hell of a tough Peruvian, that boy, and he was away and out of range before Grant could get in a second blow.

There was a slab of concrete on the ground near Diego's feet which might once have been part of the building or an outhouse or a coal bunker. He stopped quickly, picked it up in both hands and ran at Grant, holding it poised above his head. Grant used the spade like a pike to stab at Diego's stomach, but Diego stopped just out of reach and flung the concrete slab. It caught Grant a glancing blow on the right shoulder and threw him off balance. He staggered away and one foot went into the hole he had dug. He made a desperate effort to save himself, but failed and went over backwards, falling heavily.

Diego went for the concrete again. Grant looked up and saw the slab poised above him and Diego ready to crush his head with it. Sanchez had told him that Diego could break his arm, but the manservant was going further than that; it was the skull he intended breaking. But he hesitated. Maybe it had occurred to him that to kill Grant with the statuette still not found would not be quite what Mr Sanchez might have desired, or possibly he was just getting his sights lined up. Whatever the reason for that momentary hesitation, it made all the difference in the world; the difference between life and death.

Grant rolled over on to his side and took another swing with the spade, skimming the ground like a man mowing grass with a scythe. The edge of the blade caught Diego on the right shin some four inches above the ankle and there was a sharp snapping sound like a stick breaking. He gave a little howl like a whipped dog and dropped the concrete and sat down suddenly. Grant stood up and tapped him on the head with the flat of the spade and that was that; no more trouble from Diego.

He walked over to where Brad was lying, picked up the pistol and stowed it in his pocket. He was feeling pretty sick himself, with the pain in his leg and his shoulder, but he had work to do and it would not get done if he stood around massaging the sore parts of his body. So he took the roll of insulation tape from his pocket and before long he had Brad and Diego neatly trussed up and gagged with their own handkerchiefs.

It was a tough job dragging them to the car and getting them into the back, and he was in half a mind to leave them where they were and let the police find them. But he decided not to, because the coppers might just let them go, or somebody else might, and Brad for one was best kept strictly under restraint. He had nothing much against Diego except a nasty kick under the hip and a glancing blow from a slab of concrete, but Diego was best out of the way for a time also;

and maybe for ever if it really came to the point.

They were beginning to come round by the time he had got them into the car, and he was not sorry about that; he was certainly not keen on having them die on him. He had never driven a Citröen before, but he got the hang of it quickly enough and five minutes later they were back in the cul-de-sac and he was opening the door of the garage.

He still had the keys of the MGB, and he started it up and backed it out onto the road. And then he drove the Citröen into the garage, made sure that Brad and Diego were sitting comfortably, and said goodbye to them.

'You'd better pray that nothing happens to me,' he said. 'Because if it does you could be here for quite a while.'

He got no answer, which was not very surprising, seeing the way they were gagged; but they both looked at him and he had seen more signs of affection in the eyes of a cobra at the Zoo. But that was the way some people were — no hint of gratitude when you had done your best for them. He walked out of the garage, locked the door and got into the MGB. There was still not a soul around.

He parked the MGB just behind the Cortina and took the cardboard box out of the boot, and everything was as quiet as if some plague had killed off all the inhabitants, leaving him as the only person still alive. But there was that light in the window of the flat, so he supposed Miss Sims was still waiting up for him and maybe getting madder all the time. He carried the box up to the second floor, and he was limping a little and the stairs were giving him hell, but he made it. He held the box under his left arm and fished for the key with his right hand and unlocked the door and let himself in. He had a feeling of having been away a long, long time, though in point of fact it was no more than six or seven hours at the most, and he wished he could have stayed now he had reached home, because all he really wanted right then was to crawl in between the sheets and let the cares of the world roll by. He knew that that was out of the question, though; there was a lot more to be done before he could even think of getting his head down, and he just had to be thankful he had managed to snatch some sleep on the way up from Westerton.

Susan Sims was there sure enough. She was sound asleep, curled up in an armchair in front of the television set, which was presenting a blank screen and giving out a faint humming sound, as though it, too, had dozed off. He put the box on the table and switched off the television and woke the girl.

'I'm home,' he said.

She blinked her eyes at him and sat up. 'Holy Motheth, Tham!' she said. 'Where have you been? What time ith it, for goodneth thake? And where ith Melitha?'

'I've been down to Westerton,' Grant said. 'It's a quarter past two and Melissa is at the Old Hall with Mr Sanchez and a man named Slicer.'

'Thlither! Who on earth ith he?'

'I have reason to believe he's the character who carved his trade-mark on the late Mr Olmedo.'

'Oh, God!' she said. 'I think you'd

better tell me all about it.'

He told her very quickly, and he could see she was not happy about it. He was not terribly happy about it himself, but an old aunt had often told him in the days of his youth that people were not brought into the world to be happy, so he supposed he ought not to grumble. She had never got round to telling him what people were brought into the world to be, so maybe she had never found out about that part of the contract. It was a pretty negative sort of philosophy, but there it was; take it or leave it.

He went to the kitchen and rummaged in a drawer and came back with a hammer and screwdriver. He laid them on the table and took the statuette out of the cardboard box while Susan Sims looked on. He turned the statuette over on to its side and examined the base. And then he saw the mark; it was scarcely noticeable, but it was there; a tiny indentation near the edge, so inconspicuous that nobody who was not specifically searching for something of the kind would ever have found it. He had overlooked it himself the first time round. He gave a sigh.

'So they were different.'

'Different?'

'The two statuettes. This one is something special.'

'What'th tho thpethial about it?'

'I don't know. But I intend to find out.'

He began to scrape at the base with the screwdriver, but the material was hard and he was making little impression. He picked up the hammer and began to chip away at the statuette, using the screwdriver as a cold chisel.

'What are you doing?' Miss Sims demanded. 'Have you gone crathy?'

'I sincerely hope not. I'm looking for something.'

'Like what, for inthtanth?'

'Like gold maybe.'

'Now I know you're crathy,' she said.

He was not really expecting to find gold, though it was a faint possibility lurking at the back of his mind. The fact that there had been no appreciable difference in weight between the two statuettes did not rule it out; they could have been made to match up in that respect as in all others so that it would be impossible to pick one out from a batch except by means of that tiny and almost invisible mark on the base. Yet he knew that this was still only conjecture and that the final result of his work with the hammer and screwdriver might be nothing more profitable than one slightly damaged representation of an Inca prince. But there had to be something about this particular statuette which made it valuable; Olmedo had said it was and Sanchez had confirmed the fact by going to such lengths to gain possession of it. So what made it so rich a prize?

He had soon given up the idea of its being golden under the outer crust, but he went on chipping away and suddenly the screwdriver penetrated the base and went in to a depth of about an inch. He pulled it out and a trickle of white powder flowed on to the table from the hole it had made. There was some of the powder adhering to the screwdriver also.

'Well now,' he said, 'Who would have believed it? The stuff you find inside these objects of art.' He took up a little of the powder on his forefinger and touched it with the tip of his tongue. It had a bitter taste and he wiped his tongue with his handkerchief.

'What ith it?' Susan Sims asked.

'Well, it isn't salt and it isn't icing-sugar,' Grant said. 'I'm not an expert on these things, so I can't be absolutely certain, but bearing in mind the country of origin, I'd be prepared to stick my neck out and make a bet that it's snow.'

'Thnow! How can it be? It ithn't even melting.'

'Not that kind of snow, my love. Powdered cocaine. The stuff people inject into their bloodstream or maybe sniff up their noses to make them happy. Only it doesn't, not for long.'

She looked startled and a bit scared. 'Oh, my goodneth, Tham, you really have got yourthelf micthed up in thomething now, haven't you?'

'I think I really have,' he said. 'And I think I need a cup of good strong coffee. Be a darling and make some, will you?'

She went off to the kitchen, still looking

worried, and when she came back with the coffee the statuette was lying in pieces on the table and with the debris were some polythene bags of the white powder, one of them slightly damaged by the screwdriver.

'Well, at least we know now,' he said, 'that Olmedo was telling Melissa the truth. He was certainly not fooling when he said this joker was valuable. With that amount of junk inside it, it had to be.'

Susan Sims handed him one of the cups of coffee and sipped a little from the other. 'How much ith it worth, do you think?'

Grant also drank some coffee — and he needed it, he really did. 'I believe,' he said, 'that the going rate on the black market — which is obviously where this little lot was meant to go — is something over a thousand pounds an ounce, and it's going up all the time. I'd say we have here maybe ten or twelve pounds. Let's make it a nice round figure and call it a quarter of a million.'

She stared at him, her eyes popping. 'A quarter of a million poundth thterling?'

'Don't quote me,' Grant said. 'It's just a guess. But whatever the sum is, it's a hell of a lot.'

'What was Mr Olmedo doing with it?'

'Ah, well, that's another question. I'm afraid our sweet Melissa's Latin lover was something of a crook, and the legitimate side of the business was just a cover for a far more lucrative trade. It also seems he fell out with his cousin Guido over some financial matter, and that, for him, was where the trouble started. Because Guido is just as much a crook as Enrique ever was, and maybe even more so. I think Olmedo intended selling this consignment on the side to settle the account with Sanchez. Only he never got round to doing it because events caught up with him and he ended up dead. Dear Cousin Guido employed a couple of hard boys to pick up the missing portion and we know how they went to work.'

'What will you do now?'

'I shall have to contact the police of course.'

'You ought to have done that before.'

'I know. You don't have to tell me.' He

swallowed the rest of the coffee and it was far too hot and burnt his mouth. 'But better late than never. I'll get Walden on the blower.'

'He'll be in bed.'

'Then he'll have to get out of bed.'

'He'll be pleathed.'

'I don't give a damn whether he's pleased or not. I'm not in bed, am I? So why should he be? It's his case.'

'Well,' she said, 'if you put it like that . . . '

13

Strange Weed

Detective Sergeant Edgar Walden, roused from his well-earned slumber in the small hours of the morning, was certainly not pleased. Grant had managed with a certain amount of difficulty and some slight prevarication to obtain his home number from Scotland Yard, and had then dialled it without further delay. When he gave his name he thought Walden sounded as though he were choking.

'You! Do you know what time it is?'

'I know. But this is important.'

'It had better be.'

'I've found the lady.'

'Miss Lloyd?'

'Yes.'

'In the middle of the night?'

'Last night, actually.'

Walden did some more choking. 'Damn you, Sam; you were holding out on us. What else have you been doing, you bastard?'

'I've been finding the men who killed Olmedo.'

This time he thought Walden must be throwing a fit or something; it was a few minutes before be became coherent again, and it seemed to have taken a great effort of self-control. 'You'd better let me have it. All of it. Every bloody detail.'

Grant gave him all of it — in condensed form. He was aware of time slipping away and he kept thinking of Melissa down at Westerton Old Hall with Sanchez and Slicer.

'Is that the lot?' Walden asked in a strictly controlled voice when he had finished.

'That's the lot.'

'You haven't forgotten anything?'

'Nothing.'

'Right, then. Stay where you are. Don't move out of that flat. You understand?'

'But — '

'Damn you, Sam; do what I say or by God you'll be for the high jump.'

Walden rang off then. Grant heard the

rattle of the receiver going down. He hung up and went back to the sitting room.

'Did you get him?' Susan Sims asked.

'Yes, I got him.'

'What did he say?'

'He told me to stay right here.'

'And are you going to do that?'

'No; I'm going back to Westerton.'

'Oh, no, Tham. Leave it to the polithe.'

'I don't know how long they'll take to get there, and I don't trust Sanchez and Slicer. There'll be somebody coming along to pick that up, I expect.' He pointed at the bags of white powder. 'Let them in.' He laid the keys of the MGB and the key of the lock-up garage on the table. 'You'd better give them these too. They'll be needing them.'

'But, Tham — '

He gave her a quick kiss. 'I'll be back.'

'But — '

He was out of the flat before she could raise any further objection. He was still limping a bit and his right shoulder ached, but he made it to ground floor in quick time and he got into the Cortina and started the engine. He put the thing in gear and pulled away from the red MGB parked astern, and he was thinking that there was something of a shuttle service going on between his flat and Westerton these days. But not much longer maybe; maybe it was all getting very near the end now.

He really pushed the Cortina as soon as he got clear of London, and he was not giving a damn about the speed limit. He had the side windows open and was letting cool air flow in, because if he fell asleep now he was going to be in real trouble. He was in trouble enough as it was, and he was going to have a lot of talking to do and a lot of explaining in order to get himself out of it; but if he went to sleep at the wheel of a car travelling at eighty miles an hour or more, that would be the end of everything — for him.

It was beginning to grow light when he arrived at Westerton, but nobody was moving in the village as far as he could see. He turned off down the lane with the beech trees on either side and a little later he was at the gates. He took the Cortina into the drive and left it there just inside the gateway on the grass verge and went the rest of the way on foot. He had about a couple of hundred yards to go, and he got off the drive and made a detour, keeping under cover as much as possible in order not to be seen from the house if anyone was keeping a watch. He could feel the weight of Brad's pistol in his pocket and he hoped he would not have to use it; he hoped that a threat would be enough. All he wanted was to keep Sanchez and Slicer quiet until the police arrived — if they were not there already. He had seen no police cars around, so it rather looked as though they were not. It would take Walden a bit of time to get things organised; there would be the question of warrants and so on. He had certainly done the right thing in coming down without delay.

He came out by the swimming-pool; the house was a grey mass beyond it. He could see the side windows of the big drawing room, but the curtains were still drawn and there was no sign of any life.

Perhaps the two men had gone to bed after having locked Melissa in one of the other rooms. It was possible, but he thought it was unlikely; he doubted whether Sanchez would be able to rest until he had his hands on the statuette. Not that he ever would have his hands on it now.

The tiles round the swimming-pool were wet; it could have been dew or the rain that had fallen the previous evening and had still not dried off. Certainly it was not likely that anyone had been taking an early morning swim and splashing water on the tiles. In fact it was doubtful whether anyone had used the pool since the previous summer. Maybe Olmedo and Melissa had played around in it then, enjoying themselves the way Olmedo for one would never enjoy himself again. Nor was it likely that Melissa would ever again swim in that particular pool; all that was finished as far as she was concerned; she had had her good times at the Old Hall but they were over now, over and done with, never to return.

He walked round by the far end where the diving-boards were, keeping a wary eye on the house in case Sanchez or Slicer should appear, but he had still caught no glimpse of any movement. He paused with one hand resting on the rail of the ladder leading up to the high diving-board, looking towards the house and thinking out what move to make. If the front door was not locked it would be simple enough to walk in with the pistol in his hand and confront the two men. He could then keep an eye on them until the police turned up. Melissa would be relieved to see him; that was certain. There was, of course, Slicer's flick-knife to beware of, but he would see to it that Slicer had no opportunity to use it. Sanchez might possibly have a gun, but he doubted it; Sanchez was the kind of man who preferred to have others to do his dirty work for him.

But supposing the door was locked. What then? Ring the bell? Slicer would probably be sent to open the door and he could ram the pistol into Slicer's belly and take the knife from him. After that he could deal with Sanchez. At least, that was the way it might go if all went well; but he had had too much experience of such matters to kid himself that all would necessarily go well; there were always unforeseen snags to foul things up.

Still, he had to make a move of some kind, and he could think of no better plan, so he took his hand off the rail and got going. He had reached the corner of the pool on the other side of the diving structure when he caught sight of something hanging on the ladder which led down into the water. The light was still poor and he could not quite make out what it was; it looked like some kind of weed growing there and trailing in the water, He walked to the ladder and reached down and grasped this strange weed in his hand. It came to him then with a quick sense of shock, the realisation of what in fact it was — a wig of long blonde hair.

He stood with the wig in his hand staring down into the water. It was murky with all the dirt that had silted into it, but he could see something there, motionless, lying on the bottom. And he knew what it was.

He felt a blaze of anger. So they had not waited; they had had to jump the gun. It was Slicer of course, Slicer who had done it. But Sanchez must have allowed him to; he could have prevented it if he had wished. And he had not wished. They had always intended getting rid of her, so why wait? Why not make use of the time that was lying heavy on their hands? Why not finish that part of the job without further delay? It would at least save them the bother of watching the girl.

The bastards! The damned murdering bastards! He felt a burning hatred for them, a white-hot anger at what they had done. And he knew that he himself was responsible. He had found her; he had delivered her up to Sanchez; all unwittingly he had supplied the victim. There was a bitter taste in his mouth, anguish in his mind. He had had it in his power to avert this tragedy and he had failed to do so.

He heard the sudden patter of running feet and turned a moment late. The knife slid across his ribs, cutting through cloth and skin and flesh. He uttered a gasp of sharply sucked-in breath as he felt the pain and the shock. He heard Slicer's laugh, and he stepped back and his foot went over the edge. He dropped the wig and made a grab at the ladder-rail and missed it; and then he was falling. He hit the water and went under, and he touched the girl's body and thrust himself away from it with a sense of revulsion, as though it had been something unspeakably loathsome.

When he came to the surface he saw Slicer on the edge of the pool tracing airy patterns with the knife, grinning, drooling a little.

'You killed her,' he said. 'You bloody swine, you killed her.'

Slicer laughed gloatingly. 'I 'ad 'er first, though. Nice, it was. Olmedo's fancy piece.' He smacked his moist, running lips; slobbering with the recollection. 'Nice.' It was the crowning touch; if anything more had been needed to make it utterly vile, this was it. And maybe Sanchez had had her too. One after the other — to pass the time.

Slicer grinned down at him. 'You goin' to stay in there, Sam boy?'

He was treading water, his side hurting where the knife had made that shallow cut across the ribs. He felt in his pocket and hauled out the pistol and swam to the ladder and hung on with his left hand. Slicer made a thrust at him with the knife, but he jerked his head out of range and lifted the pistol, aiming at Slicer's belly. He had one thought only in his mind — to kill Slicer. Slicer was too foul a thing to be allowed to live; he would kill the swine now and finish with it.

He pushed off the safety-catch with his thumb, and he knew there was a round in the chamber because he had made sure of that before leaving the car; not knowing that it was for Slicer, but knowing it now, knowing it so damned well.

Slicer had not moved; it was as though the sight of the gun in Grant's hand had petrified him after that one abortive stab with the knife. So he was there when Grant pressed the trigger; a mark too big to miss, a barn door of a mark. Yet no bullet entered his body; he remained unscathed, unmarked, unharmed in any way. There was a metallic clicking sound and that was all.

14

The Dirty Work

It could have been because of the water getting into the weapon and fouling things up; it could have been a simple misfire; the result either way was the same: no curtains for Slicer.

Grant swore. Slicer gave a high-pitched laugh, slightly hysterical from the relief of finding himself unharmed when he must have thought he was going to have a hole blasted into his stomach. But he recovered quickly enough from his fright and made another stab at Grant with the knife, aiming for the face. Grant jerked back again out of range and threw the pistol at Slicer. It hit him on the chin and he let out a howl; but though it had hurt him, it had inflicted no effective damage, merely serving to enrage him and goad him into taking a step forward and making another vicious thrust with the knife.

Grant flung himself backwards off the ladder and swam down to the shallow end, where he stood waist-deep in the water looking at Slicer and wondering where he could go from there. He could feel the blood flowing from the wound in his side and he was feeling pretty sick and groggy. He wanted to sit down, but he knew he had to keep standing. God, he had made a mess of things, a right flaming mess of things and no mistake.

And then he saw Sanchez come out of the house. Sanchez came over to the pool with his waddling duck's walk and stared at him.

'I see you're back.'

'There's nothing wrong with your eyesight, then,' Grant said.

Sanchez said, a crackle of anger in his voice: 'Where is the statuette? Where are Diego and the other man?'

'Safe.'

Sanchez gazed round about him as though expecting to see the two men. 'Where are they?'

'In my garage in London.'

'You've been playing tricks, Mr Grant.'

'You've been playing tricks too. You said you'd take care of the girl, but you let that damned psycho get at her.'

'She acted foolishly. She tried to run away.'

'And he ran after her?'

'What else was there to do? I could not have caught her; I am hardly built for speed.'

'But he caught her, didn't he? And you let him do as he pleased with her. Maybe you watched. Maybe you enjoyed that.'

Slicer gave a low, gurgling chuckle. It was like an obscenity. Grant felt cold and sick in the stomach; he wanted to crawl out of the water and lie down; but there was the knife in Slicer's hand tracing patterns again. Eventually, of course, Slicer would wade into the water and come to him; and then he would have to fight, feeling like death.

Sanchez said again: 'Where is the statuette?'

'I'm sorry about that,' Grant said.

'What have you done with it?'

'I hit it with a hammer — accidentally, of course. You'll never guess what there was inside. Snow, Mr Sanchez; snow in polythene bags. Your cousin was right: it was valuable. I imagine the drug department could well be working out the figures right now. It's their pigeon, you see. It's a different lot who'll be arresting you on the murder charge, of course.'

He was really feeling bad now, with all that blood dripping out of him; it was turning the water pink in the gradually strengthening light. He was not sure how much longer he could hang on.

But Slicer was looking uneasy. 'I don't like the sound of this, Mr Sanchez. I think we oughter get moving. If the fuzz is on to us they could be down 'ere soon. We better scarper.'

There was a conflict of emotions portrayed on Sanchez's face — rage, frustration, anxiety. He must have seen that events were closing in on him, and he was possibly regretting that he had ever employed Grant, a tool that had turned in his hand. What could he do now? Get out of the country? He would need to act very quickly to have any chance of doing that.

'Mr Sanchez!' Slicer's voice rose in desperation. 'We gotta go.'

'Yes,' Sanchez said, as though reaching a decision, 'we must go. But first you will kill him.' He pointed a finger at Grant. 'Do it quickly.'

Slicer looked at the water and hesitated. It was not that he shrank from the task, but he was obviously not keen on getting himself wet in the process. Yet while Grant stayed obstinately in the pool there appeared to be no other way. He glanced at Sanchez.

'You ain't got a gun?'

'No,' Sanchez said impatiently. 'Use the knife. You know how.'

Slicer apparently came to the conclusion that there was nothing else for it and lowered himself into the pool at the shallow end. He began to wade towards Grant, the knife firmly gripped in his left hand.

Grant retreated into deeper water. He wondered whether Slicer could swim, but he hardly felt like swimming himself; he was getting cramps and the blood was still flowing.

Slicer came nearer, holding the knife above water. There was a cut on his chin where the pistol had struck it; a little blood, too. Grant could see that he needed a shave. At that time in the morning he was in need of a shave himself. But he was not worrying about appearances.

'It won't do you any good,' he said. 'They'll get you anyway.'

'Maybe they will,' Slicer said, 'but I'll get you first, you bleeder.'

It was the right word, Grant thought; he was a bleeder sure enough. And before long he might be a goner.

'Hurry,' Sanchez shouted.

It was all right for him, standing on the edge and handing out his orders. He ought to come into the water and see how he liked it. Grant hoped he would not, all the same. One was enough.

Slicer made a sudden lunge, but the water impeded him and the lunge was short. He stumbled forward and Grant leaned towards him and gave him a karate chop on the back of the neck. Slicer grunted, but karate had never been one of Grant's strong suits and the way he felt just then it probably hurt him as much as it hurt Slicer; it seemed to tear something down there by the ribs where the knife had done its work.

He backed away, and there was a lot of slime on the bottom, so that it was difficult to keep his footing. He was getting nearer the deep end again and was submerged up to the top of his chest. Slicer was an inch or two shorter than he was and was getting out of his depth. Suddenly he began to swim; which settled that question, if not in the way Grant would have wished it settled. He started swimming also — away from Slicer.

But it was hurting him; every movement hurt now. He was hampered by his clothes and he could no longer keep an eye on Slicer because the knife-man, the psycho, was behind him. He headed for the ladder on which he had found the blonde wig, that pathetic little piece of disguise which had failed in the end to save Melissa. He had a half-formed idea that if he could get to the ladder before

Slicer he might somehow manage from that point to ward the man off; might even wrest the knife from his hand, though he was not sure how. But when he reached the ladder Sanchez was already there.

'No, Mr Grant, no,' Sanchez said. He put one hand on the rail to balance himself and kicked out with his left foot, catching Grant on the side of the head and adding a little more pain to go with the rest of it.

Slicer had arrived by then and he had another go with the knife; but he had no solid base from which to launch his attack and he was off target and the lunge carried him under. There was some confusion then and Grant managed to thrust off from the ladder with his feet and get out of range again. But it was all becoming very exhausting and he doubted whether he could keep it going for much longer.

He got himself down to the shallow end again and stood up. The water was streaming off him and he was shaking like a branch in a high wind. Slicer had followed him and was standing about ten feet away, getting his breath back after his exertions. Sanchez had walked along the edge of the pool and was shouting at Slicer, urging him to make haste and finish it. He sounded very impatient and it was obvious that he was aware of the pressing need to have done with the business and get away.

'What are you waiting for? You have him now. He cannot run. Kill him.'

Slicer would probably have done it without any encouragement from Sanchez; he was merely pausing a moment or two before launching another and perhaps final attack. Grant saw him brace himself and knew that this was it. He waited, not trying to avoid Slicer any more; he had done with that; now he must stand and fight — if he could.

Slicer began to move in, as if sensing that Grant had given up any thought of further retreat. Grant watched Slicer's left hand; that was the killer. Slicer was six feet away now and still Grant had not moved. Slicer gave a sneering laugh, taunting him.

'Feeling tired, Sam boy? No more running away? Too bad.'

Grant said nothing, not wasting his breath. He watched the knife. Slicer advanced another step, and another; then stopped. Grant saw the left hand start to go back ready for the thrust. He moved then, reaching out with his right hand and getting a grip on Slicer's wrist. He was carried forward by his own momentum and his chest came up against Slicer's and he thought for a moment that the two of them were going to fall; but though they staggered a little, they kept their footing.

Slicer was trying to break the grip on his wrist, but Grant looped his right arm round the back of Slicer's neck and got a second grip on it from behind. He tried to bend Slicer's arm back and maybe dislocate it, but his side was hurting like hell and he could feel the strength going out of him like sand out of a ripped sack. Slicer seemed to guess as much and he did some dirty work with his right fist below the water level, giving that lacerated flesh a lot more agony. He was laughing again, too, so it was a hundred to one he knew he was on the winning side and would finish it pretty soon.

'You've 'ad it, Sam boy. Best admit it. Give it up, Sam, an' take what's comin' to you. Give it up.'

Grant could feel his grip on Slicer's wrist weakening. It really was all up with him; he had reached the end of his tether and he knew it. The fingers of his left hand slipped from the wrist and the point of the knife shifted towards his throat. With his right hand he still held on, desperately striving to keep that bright steel blade away from him. But there was that wretched weakness in his arm, in his whole body, and it needed only the final effort from Slicer now.

But then Slicer relaxed the pressure and seemed to forget about what he had been doing. He turned his head as though listening, and it was plain that he was not happy about what he had heard. Grant heard it too, but he was happier about it. It was the sound of a car approaching up the drive from the gateway.

So the police had arrived; it could only be them. And not before time, not before they were needed. He was relieved, but he also felt a shade resentful that they should have run it so close. He might have been killed; he damned nearly had been.

He was looking towards the drive, but there was a lot of mist over in that direction and he could make out nothing but a kind of shadow travelling fast. Slicer was looking in that direction too, and so was Sanchez. And none of them was moving; it was as though the sound had frozen all three of them into the positions they had held before it had caught the ear.

The sound became clearer, and then Grant heard the car hit the gravel in front of the house and he expected it to stop there, but he was wrong; it came round the corner of the house and he knew that he had been wrong, too, about its being the police. Unless the coppers had taken to going around in red MGBs, which seemed unlikely, to say the least.

The hood was up and for the moment he was unable to see who was driving it; but he could guess. She must have caught a glimpse of the swimming-pool as she came up the drive; she must have seen what was going on, or guessed, and she had not hesitated; she had come straight on towards it, not caring a brass farthing about the shrubs and the flower-beds standing in her way, but going clean through them like a little red tank.

He thought for an instant that she was going to drive straight into the pool, carrying Sanchez with her. Sanchez must have had the same idea, and he started to run. It was a trifle late for that; he should have thought of it sooner. She hauled the MGB round, and the tyres made a screeching sound on the tiles and the tail came within an inch of sliding over the edge, but she held it; and then she was going after Sanchez like a dog after a rabbit. He got to the deep end of the pool just ahead of her and cut off to the right, but she brought the car round in a tight turn and caught him before he could make it to the trees.

It was the offside front wing that hit him and it broke his hip. He gave a shriek and went down, and stayed down, moaning. She just left him there and brought the MGB back to the other side of the pool and got out and looked at the two men standing in the water. Grant had released Slicer's wrist and had backed away from him; but Slicer was not trying to do anything in the knife line; both he and Grant had watched the girl chasing Sanchez with a kind of awed fascination. It had all taken less than half a minute from the time when they had first heard the sound of the car, and it had finished Sanchez.

But the knife was still in Slicer's hand.

Susan Sims stood on the edge of the pool looking as cool as if nothing whatever out of the ordinary had occurred; as cool and fresh as the morning air, and ten times as welcome.

'Are you all right, Tham?' she asked.

'No,' Grant said. 'I've been knifed and I'm bleeding and I feel like death.' Why lie about it? Why try to fob her off with assurances that he was as fit as a flea when he was as sick as a spavined louse?

She switched her gaze to Slicer and she was not so cool any more. In fact she was as angry as Grant had ever seen her. 'You damned thwine,' she cried. 'I'll thee you pay for thith if it'th the latht thing I do. Ath God ith my witneth, I will.'

He wondered why it was that she always had to get so theatrical in her language in situations such as this. He was afraid it came from watching all those old films on television and picking up the dialogue. And it was hardly likely to impress a man like Slicer.

It didn't. He just laughed. He seemed to be a lot happier now that he could see he had only a girl to deal with. And not a big, hefty, hockey-playing, horse-riding Amazon either, but a sweet little slip of a thing in pale green slacks and a pale green sweater. Why should he worry?

'Lady,' he said, 'you won't do nothin' to me.' He pointed at Grant with the knife. 'And 'e may feel bad now, but 'e won't feel nothin' much longer. I'm going to finish 'im, finish 'im for good an' all; an' you ain't stopping me.'

'Drop the knife,' she said. 'You hear me?'

He ignored the order and began to

wade towards Grant. Grant moved away towards the deeper water, and it all seemed to be happening again like the repeat of a bad dream. Slicer obviously intended to kill him in spite of what had happened; and then maybe he would go for the girl and finally take the MGB to get away from there. He was not likely to do anything for Sanchez, who was still lying where he had fallen and groaning now and then as though in a great deal of pain.

'Why don't you go now?' Grant said. 'You're wasting valuable time. Don't you know that?'

Slicer shook his head. 'I got time. I finish what I start.' There was a crazy look in his eyes. He was a psycho sure enough. He probably loved killing for its own sake and would stay and do it even if it meant getting caught. It was hopeless trying to reason with such a man.

Grant was feeling really weak; his head was swimming and he could not get away from Slicer. Slicer had him, was just savouring the moment, choosing with unhurried deliberation the spot to strike.

Then Susan Sims came in again. 'Drop it,' she said, 'or I'll drill you.'

They both turned their heads and looked at her, and Grant saw that she had picked up the pistol which he had thrown at Slicer. She was holding it in both hands and aiming it at the man.

Slicer gave another jeering laugh. 'You can put that away, girlie. It don't work.'

'We'll thee about that,' she said. 'If you don't drop the knife pronto we'll really thee about that.'

Slicer just turned his back on her contemptuously.

'Okay,' she said. 'You athked for it.' And then she pressed the trigger and shot Slicer in the arm.

He gave a screech and dropped the knife; it fell with a faint plopping sound into the water and vanished from sight.

'Now,' Miss Sims said, 'you'd better come out of there.'

She had to give Grant some help in climbing out; he doubted whether he could have done it on his own. She let Slicer get out as best he could without assistance. He managed to do so, and then he sat down rather suddenly, nursing his left arm. There was a lot of blood running down the hand and dripping from the ends of the fingers.

Grant said: 'I don't know how you got the gun to work. It wouldn't for me.'

She just smiled in a superior kind of way, and he remembered then that she knew just about all there was to know about Walther PPKs because she had once had a German boy friend who had been a bit of a gun nut and had given her lessons on that subject in between the bouts of athletic love-making. Maybe the trouble had been no more than a simple misfire after all, and she had merely worked the slide and put another round into the chamber.

'I thought I told you to wait at the flat,' he said.

'You ought to be glad I didn't. You'd have been in a nithe ficth if I had. Where ith Melitha?'

'They killed her.'

'Oh, no! Oh, God, no!'

'I just wasn't in time.'

She looked sick about it and he thought

for a moment she was going to cry, but she pulled herself together and started doing something about the cut that Slicer's knife had inflicted. She got him out of his jacket and tore his shirt away, and it seemed pretty foul with the blood just about everywhere and still coming out like water from a leaky tank. But it probably looked worse than it was. He hoped so anyway; he certainly hoped so.

It was lucky she was not the sort who fainted at the sight of blood or any of that nonsense. In fact she was a lot more capable in an emergency than most people would have believed; she was not just something decorative to have around the house. So when she had got the shirt torn away she took one look at the wound and said she would have to go to the house and get something for a dressing.

She left him the gun so that he could keep an eye on Slicer; but Slicer was just moaning and not likely to make any more trouble. Sanchez had still not moved from the place where he had been knocked down, and it was all rather like a battlefield with the wounded lying around and waiting for the stretcher-bearers to come along.

Susan Sims was not gone for long. She came back with a clean sheet and a pair of scissors, and she made a very workmanlike job of the bandaging, so that he began to think he might live after all.

She had just finished when the police arrived. It was like them, he thought, to turn up after all the dirty work had been done.

15

Something Useful

'You needn't expect any thanks from me,' Detective Sergeant Walden said.

'I paid for the beer,' Grant reminded him.

'I wasn't referring to the beer; I know you're only trying to buy me off. No; I was referring to that job you had to go sticking your nose in.'

'It was all cleared up very nicely, I thought.'

'It would have been cleared up a lot more nicely if you'd done what I told you.'

'Is that the way Kerrison feels?'

'Never mind how he feels. You're damned lucky nobody is bringing charges against you. Lucky to be alive, too, I'd say. How's that knife job coming along?'

'You really mean you're interested in my state of health?' Grant asked.

'I have to inquire. It's expected.'

'Well, since you're so solicitous, I'll tell you it's coming along very nicely. Of course, I wouldn't want anyone to give me a dig in the ribs just yet, and I have to mind how I laugh, but it isn't nearly as bad as I thought it might be.'

'It'll leave a scar, though,' Walden said; and he seemed to take some small comfort from that reflection.

'But not where people are likely to see it.'

'Except maybe Miss Sims.'

'She saw it when it was new.'

'Now there,' Walden said, 'is a very smart young lady, if you want my opinion.'

'I'd love to have your opinion,' Grant said. 'And I bet she would too.'

'If it hadn't been for her I don't reckon you'd be alive right now to buy me another pint.'

'I don't suppose I should.'

'Where did she learn to handle a gun?'

'Now that's a rather long and sordid story.'

'They're the sort I like,' Walden said.

'And incidentally, did I tell you who used to own that particular weapon?'

'No, you didn't.'

'Well, it's a funny thing but it was registered in the name of Mr Enrique Olmedo.'

'I rather thought it might be.'

Walden looked sour. 'You know everything, don't you? You ought to be a copper.'

'I used to be, remember?'

Walden drank some more beer. 'If you really want thanks you should try the drug boys.'

'You think so?'

'You put them on to something, didn't you? Sanchez and Olmedo had a very nice little business on the go with that Olsan-Peru Import-Export caper. They must really have made a packet on those Inca statuettes; the marked ones, I mean. And then they had to go and foul it all up just because one cousin thought he'd been cheated by the other.'

'Some people get very annoyed when they think they're being cheated. Have any of the distributors been picked up?'

‘A number of people are helping the police with their inquiries. And strictly between ourselves, friend Sanchez is singing like a lark. I suppose he thinks it may help him.’

‘Well,’ Grant said, ‘I’m glad I was able to be of some assistance to the forces of law and order. If you should ever need my services again you have only to ask. I’ll be only too happy to step into the breach.’

Walden stared at him balefully. ‘Just try it, mate; just try it.’

* * *

Mr Peking looked up from some papers he was reading when Grant walked in. He gave a flip of the hand to indicate a chair and invited Grant to sit down. Grant thanked him and did so.

‘I trust the — ah — injury is progressing satisfactorily.’

‘It’s doing very nicely,’ Grant said.

‘I’m glad to hear it. A nasty business, that, very nasty. Frankly, Grant, I don’t like having my investigators carved up with knives — or any other sharp implements if it comes to that.'

'I don't think your investigators care very much for it either.'

'No? Well, perhaps not. All the same, you should bear in mind how much it upsets our routine to have any of you on the sick list.'

'I'll remember that in future.'

'I wish you would.'

Mr Peking gave a deep sigh, as though another distasteful subject had come into his mind. 'I have been looking back through your record, Grant, and I have discovered a most unfortunate tendency.'

'And that is?'

'A surprisingly high proportion of your clients have turned out to be of a criminal — not to say homicidal — character.'

'I don't choose the clients,' Grant said.

'Nevertheless — '

'And I believe they've all paid up like honest citizens. Even better than some honest citizens.'

Mr Peking brightened perceptibly. 'Do you know, Grant, that's a very shrewd observation, very shrewd indeed. So they have, to be sure.'

‘So maybe it would pay us to keep an eye open for a few more crooks to work for.’

Mr Peking frowned. ‘Now, Grant, there’s no need to go as far as that. If we act on behalf of crooks in the mistaken belief that they are persons of strict integrity and indubitable moral fibre, that is one thing. To take up with people whom we know only too well to be on the wrong side of the law would be quite a different kettle of fish. By Jupiter, yes.’

‘I suppose so.’

Mr Peking sighed once again, more gustily than ever. ‘Regarding your expense account, there is a certain item which I quite fail to understand.’ He shuffled the papers in front of him. ‘Ah, here it is. One Inca pottery statuette, price twenty-five pounds. How, may I ask, was that essential to your inquiry?’

‘For purposes of comparison.’

‘Comparison with what?’

‘Another Inca statuette.’

‘I think you had better explain.’

Grant explained.

‘So you are telling me it was necessary

for you to buy this — ah — article in order to find out what Mr Sanchez was up to?'

'Yes.'

'Yet, as I understand it, you were not being employed to find out what he was up to. You were supposed to be looking for a certain young lady who had disappeared.'

'That's true, but the statuette came into it.'

'And where is this object now?'

'The police have got it.'

'Ah!' Mr Peking's face creased into a satisfied smile. 'Then my advice to you, Grant, is to go to the police and ask them to pay you your twenty-five pounds.'

He picked up a pen and with an air of the greatest satisfaction drew a thick black line through the item on the expense account.

* * *

Grant sat on the linen hamper and looked at Miss Sims with her hair tied in a knot on top of her head.

‘You look very beautiful in the bath, Susie darling.’

‘Only in the bath, Tham?’

‘In or out. Always beautiful. You’re not going to walk out on me, are you?’

‘In thith thtate? I’d be arrethted.’

‘In any state.’

‘Goodneth me,’ she said, ‘why would I do that? Don’t you know a girl mutht have an older man to give her a thenth of thecurity?’

‘Is that all I am to you — a sense of security?’

‘Not all, Tham. That’th jutht a part of it. There are many other fathetth to my need for you.’

‘You must tell me about those other facets some day. It sounds a fascinating subject. But you told me once a girl needed a younger man.’

‘Now you’re throwing that in my teeth again.’

‘I’m sorry.’

‘And anyway,’ she said, ‘who would look after you if I didn’t? You need me, Tham.’

‘I know.’

She rippled the water with her toes and looked thoughtful. 'I liked her, you know.'

'Who?' Grant asked.

'Melitha, of courthe.'

'Even though she was a stripper?'

'That wath forthed on her. And it wath all patht and done with anyway.'

'Once a stripper always a stripper. That's what you say.'

'There can be an exthepthion, can't there?'

'And she was an exception?'

'Yeth.'

'I thought when I brought her here you were going to throw her out. Or throw a tantrum.'

'Well, it wath a bit much, wathn't it?'

'I didn't think you were here.'

'And what if I hadn't been? Would you have gone to bed with her?'

'Certainly not. It was a strictly professional relationship.'

He thought she was going to pursue the subject, but she let it drop. She did some more water-rippling with her toes.

Then she said: 'That man at the commune — the one with the thotgun

— he wath in love with her, wathn't he?'

'She said he thought he was.'

'Don't you think we ought to go down there and thee him?'

'I don't think I should be very welcome. I was the one who took her away.'

'You muthn't blame yourthelf for that. They would have found her thometime. It wath inevitable.'

'Maybe it was.'

Nevertheless, he did blame himself. He had done it the wrong way, all the wrong way, and the girl was dead. He knew he could never go down to the commune and explain to the young man who had loved her. No, he could never do that. What could he say to him?

Miss Sims broke in on his meditation. 'If you really want to do thomething utheful,' she said, 'you can thcrub my back. Only gently, Tham, very gently.'

He got up from the linen hamper, walked over to the bath and began to do something useful.

Other titles in the
Linford Mystery Library:

DEATH IN RETREAT

George Douglas

On a day of retreat for clergy at Overdale House, a resident guest, Martin Pender, is foully murdered. The primary task of the Regional Homicide Squad is to track down the bogus parson who joined the retreat. Subsequent events show that serious political motives lie behind the killing, but the basic lead to it all is missing. Then, three young tearaways corner the killer in the woods, and a chess problem, set out on a board, yields vital evidence.

THE DEAD DON'T SCREAM

Leonard Gribble

Why had a woman screamed in Knightsbridge? Anthony Slade, the Yard's popular Commander of X2, sets out to investigate. Furthering the same end is Ken Surridge, a PR executive from a Northern consortium. Like Slade, Surridge wants to know why financier Shadwell Staines was shot and why a very scared girl appeared wearing a woollen house-coat. Before any facts can be discovered the girl takes off and Surridge gives chase, with Slade hot on his heels . . .

THE CALIGARI COMPLEX

Basil Copper

Mike Faraday, the laconic L.A. private investigator, is called in when macabre happenings threaten the Martin-Hannaway Corporation. Fires, accidents and sudden death are involved; one of the partners, James Hannaway, inexplicably fell off a monster crane. Mike is soon entangled in a web of murder, treachery and deceit and through it all a sinister figure flits; something out of a nightmare. Who is hiding beneath the mask of Cesare, the somnambulist? Mike has a tough time finding out.